A SUSPECT VOW

Major Adam Canfield assured Reggie that theirs would be a marriage in name only—a device to preserve her respectability when they made their journey through the mountains alone together.

But now doubts assailed Reggie as she stood with this handsome stranger before the altar and heard the ceremony unfold. Those doubts grew stronger when he and then she said, "I do," and Adam's grip tightened on her and then his lips came down on hers.

There was nothing sham about the fire she felt in that kiss—and nothing sham about the response that surged up in her, catching her by shocking surprise.

How could she imagine that she could trust this hard and daring man in the nights that lay ahead of them beyond the boundaries of all that was safe and secure?

And even more troubling, how could she trust herself . . . ?

SIGNET REGENCY ROMANCE
COMING IN AUGUST 1993

Elizabeth Jackson
Galatea's Revenge

Barbara Allister
A Moment of Madness

Evans Porter
Sweet Lavender

The Reluctant Heroine

by

Dawn Lindsey

A SIGNET BOOK

SIGNET
Published by the Penguin Group
Penguin Books USA Inc., 375 Hudson Street,
New York, New York 10014, U.S.A.
Penguin Books Ltd, 27 Wrights Lane,
London W8 5TZ, England
Penguin Books Australia Ltd, Ringwood,
Victoria, Australia
Penguin Books Canada Ltd, 10 Alcorn Avenue,
Toronto, Ontario, Canada M4V 3B2
Penguin Books (N.Z.) Ltd, 182-190 Wairau Road,
Auckland 10, New Zealand

Penguin Books Ltd, Registered Offices:
Harmondsworth, Middlesex, England

First published by Signet,
an imprint of New American Library,
a division of Penguin Books USA Inc.

First Printing, July, 1993
10 9 8 7 6 5 4 3 2 1

 REGISTERED TRADEMARK—MARCA REGISTRADA

Printed in the United States of America

Chapter 1

June, 1812
Burgos

MAJOR ADAM CANFIELD, of His Majesty's 7th Hussars, ambled along in the wake of a clumsy cart smelling of onions and a stout peasant driving his pigs to market, and acknowledged ruefully to himself that this was always the worst part. Once he was past the guards at the gates, the rest would be relatively easy; but there was always the risk that the French sentries would be more alert than usual, and his masquerade would be undone before it had begun. If so, he faced imprisonment and probably a speedy hanging, for the French were not known for their tolerant treatment of spies.

But then his chance of being unmasked was relatively slim. He doubted if even his own men would recognize him in his present guise. Gone were the smart pelisse and silver lace so admired by Spanish señoritas and so devilish hard to obtain in the Peninsula. Gone also was the crisp air of authority and the unmistakable intelligence in the straightforward blue eyes. In their place was a Spanish peasant shuffling down the dusty road toward the gates of Burgos, with nothing more pressing on his mind than the week's shopping and a drink or two in a local taverna.

The major did not think of himself as an actor, but like an actor he understood that his success—and frequently his life—depended upon his becoming the character he had assumed. The clothes might proclaim the Spanish peasant, but the slightest slip could betray him. Expression, walk, voice, everything had to fit the part he was playing, for far more than his own life depended upon the success of his disguise. The information he brought back was frequently vital to the Allied cause, and might mean the difference between success and failure and the lives of thousands of troops.

He was helped by the fact that after nearly four years in the Peninsula he was as dark as any Spaniard and spoke Spanish like a native. With his dark curly hair and sleepy blue eyes, which in the north of Spain were by no means uncommon and could assume an expression of the blankest stupidity at will, he seldom drew a second glance, even from the most alert of the French guards. He was admittedly tall to pass for a Spaniard, but he had learned long ago that a slouch and a vacant expression worked wonders.

The two guards on duty at the gates proved no exception. The major passed through unchallenged, and he breathed a sigh of relief as the guards lounged at their post. They were frankly uninterested in the stream of peasants coming in to market, despite the fact that Burgos had long been the French emperor's direct line of communication with his Grand Armée in Spain. The country was nominally under the command of his brother, King Joseph, but in reality the army was headed by a trio of squabbling marshalls. Napoleon, busy in eastern Europe, as yet saw no threat in Lord Wellington's ragtag army, with its unhelpful Spanish and Portuguese allies, and he spared little thought and less money on the defense of Spain.

Which was exactly what Lord Wellington was counting on. After bloody and costly victories at Ciudad Rodrigo and Badajoz earlier that year, the road was now open for the British to invade Spain at long last. But Marmont reputedly still had fifty thousand seasoned troops, Soult another sixty thousand, the French Army of the North forty thousand, and Joseph's Army of the Centre at least the same. Against this enemy concentration, his lordship could bring only fifty-four guns and sixty-six thousand men, many of them worn out after four years of campaigning in a hostile climate, or weakened by the ever-present fever. That did not dismay his lordship, of course, for he was used to overwhelming odds. But it made news of the enemy's plans and fortifications even more essential.

Once inside the town, it was easy enough for the major to lose himself in the main square, for the town, long inured to the hated French soldiers and the French commandant set over them, was clearly that day thinking only of business. The French army had a deplorable habit of living off the land it invaded, and most of the riches of Spain had long since been plundered by King Joseph or his marshals; but life must go on, and crops made and eggs and milk sold.

Adam, in his guise as local peasant, ambled unremarked through the busy market, buying a loaf of bread from an ancient crone all in rusty black, and a round of cheese from a pretty girl with flashing eyes, who smiled invitingly at him and looked disappointed when he passed on without taking up her invitation. The town betrayed its conquered status by the French soldiers visible everywhere in their distinctive blue uniforms, strolling in the streets or shopping in the market. The citizens of Burgos seemed to give them a wide berth, and the major prudently followed their example, reflecting that the nearest Englishman was a hard day's ride to the south, and he could not afford to slip up.

He was mistaken. There was another English person in the market that day. Miss Regina Alderstock, long a resident of the town, was doing her weekly shopping.

Had the major but known it, she was a far more conspicuous figure in the market than he was, for well-bred Spanish women did not expose themselves to the hustle and bustle of the streets. But since she liked the cheerful confusion of the market and refused to be bound by the local antiquated customs, she had long blithely ignored the many stares she received, and by now was resignedly accepted by the residents of Burgos, who, like most Spaniards, thought all foreigners crazy anyway.

Reggie might find many things to admire in the Spanish culture, especially the sensible way they had adapted to their climate, which on a June day like that one could be brutal. But she herself had no patience with sleeping in the middle of the day, and had long ago realized that the habitual Spanish indolence was not for her. And so she continued to ride out unescorted from the town, shop freely in the marketplace, and manage her stepfather's household in an energetic manner that frequently bewildered the servants and amazed her more delicate stepsister.

Conchita, reared in the rigid protocol of the true Hidalgo class, bore her stepsister's vagaries in gentle silence, even though she herself remained perfectly content with the activities deemed suitable for a gently reared Spanish female. These generally included nothing more strenuous than the most delicate of needlework and the exchange of idle gossip with the other women of the household, both conducted while consuming an astonishing quantity of sweetmeats and cups of chocolate; then there was a long siesta in the middle of the afternoon to fortify oneself for an evening spent in the same far from exhausting pursuits, and occasionally a gentle stroll along the fashionable promenade for exercise. It went without saying that no upper class Spanish lady ventured out without being heavily veiled, to protect her delicate complexion against the ravages of the sun as well as ogling glances, and accompanied by a duenna to ward off any unwelcome advances.

Reggie knew she would quickly have gone mad if forced to lead such a life. But since she and her stepsister were genuinely fond of each other, in the interest of peace they had long ago agreed to remain politely uncritical of a way of life each found baffling, and so they remained on the best of terms.

On that day Reggie had a number of purchases to make, and then she had promised Father Gregorio she would arrange the flowers for the altar. She was not herself a Catholic, but had not hesitated to extend her energy to that sphere as well, to the frequent amusement of the aging cleric who presided there and possessed an admirably tolerant spirit. He had accepted her into his fold without question, and he frequently made use of her common sense and willingness to help, while making no attempt to convert her to his own faith. He watched in quiet amusement her attempts to help and even bully his most hapless parishioners into improving the state of abject poverty and lethargy they lived in.

All in all, it was a satisfying life. Certainly on that morning she went cheerfully about her errands, also oblivious to the presence of another Englishman within the town walls, and with not the least premonition of the dramatic turn her life was soon to take.

The major had also spent a productive morning. During the course of it he had acquired, in addition to the bread and cheese he had bought, enough parcels to make it look as if he had done his weekly shopping, all of which he would discard once safely outside of the town, along with most of the information he had come for. The open state of the town told him the French were very far from perceiving the present British threat, and the talk he had overheard gave him a pretty fair picture of the true state of the relationship between the conquered and their conquerors. In the case of an all-out assault on the town, the citizens of Burgos were likely to welcome a British victory, but unlikely to do much to bring it about.

And his military knowledge told him Burgos would be a hard nut to crack without inside help. Because of the importance of the town to French communications, and the proximity of superior French forces to come to its aid, he did not think it would be taken without a major effort, and the walls could be made nearly indefensible. Indeed, he saw some evidence that an effort to add to the fortifications was even now taking place.

The memory of the brutal and costly assaults on both Ciudad Rodrigo and Badajoz, the most bloody and horrible of the long Peninsula campaign, was still too fresh in his memory to make him welcome another such siege. They were the only battles of his long career he would not willingly have fought again; and even inured as he was to death and destruction, the atrocities that went on after the reducing of both towns still made his blood run cold. But whether his lordship meant ultimately to launch an assault on Burgos, or was merely covering all potential possibilities, as he was famed for doing, was naturally not information the major had been made privy to. It was enough for him to gather what information he could and return safely with it, if at all possible.

He continued to stroll leisurely through the crowd, looking the very picture of bucolic enjoyment, as if there were nothing more pressing on his mind than the possibility of finding a bargain or ogling a pretty girl. But underneath, every sense was on the stretch, as it had been from the moment of entering the town. He still had to get safely out of it again, and the intelligence officer who let his attention slip for even a second was too frequently a dead one. The major did not mean to add his number to the ranks if he could help it.

It was then that the absurd mishap occurred. He had almost reached the gates again when the narrow street he was making his way down proved to be completely blocked by a heavy cart jackknifed in the middle of it. It contained a load of lumber no doubt intended for the fortification work, for it was under the escort of a small troop of French soldiers, whose lieutenant looked both annoyed and impatient at the delay, and was shouting orders to the impassive Spanish muleteer in execrable Spanish.

The latter, muttering under his breath for providence to

spare him from the thrice-cursed French, was completely ignoring him and making very little headway in righting his cart.

Some little crowd of local citizens had gathered, complaining of the obstacle in the road and using the opportunity to roundly abuse the soldiers. All in all it was a volatile scene, and cursing at the delay, the major was about to retrace his steps, which would take him annoyingly out of his way, when the cart, balanced only precariously at best and badly loaded, began to topple.

There were several persons close enough to be in danger, including a ragged urchin of some six or seven, who had drawn close to the tail of the cart out of curiosity and who was in imminent danger of being crushed to death. Later the major was to regret that second's reflex, for his information was vital enough he should not have risked its not getting through, whatever the consequences. But now he reacted instinctively. He gave a shout of warning and dived for the child, still wholly unaware of his danger.

..
Chapter 2

REGGIE, making her way home laden with the more portable of her purchases, arrived on the scene just before the cart toppled. She saw the crowd gathered ahead of her and frowned a little, for it was obvious trouble was brewing. Angry voices could be heard, and there was a rising murmur of discontent from those nearest her in the little crowd.

A delicately bred female would doubtless have turned back at that point to avoid so volatile a scene. As an Englishwoman in an enemy-occupied town in a country torn by war, she had double the reason for not inviting trouble. But being of a curious nature, and not one to scorn a little personal risk in the interests of averting a nasty incident, Reggie continued determinedly on her way.

It did not take her long to grasp the important elements of the little scene. A cart had been wedged into the middle of the road, neither able to go forward or backward, and completely blocking the narrow way to both vehicles and pedestrians. It was by no means an unusual occurrence in that town of winding streets scarcely wide enough for a single vehicle to pass, and closely hedged on both sides by the whitewashed walls of the buildings. The only thing that made this scene in any way remarkable was the presence of the small troop of French soldiers escorting the cart.

By and large the Spanish and French managed to live together in an uneasy peace. The French were contemptuous of the Spanish and seldom troubled to hide it, and the citizens of the town deeply hated their French conquerors. But the war had been going on so many years by then that affairs seldom broke out into open conflict.

The present scene could quickly turn ugly, however. At present the French lieutenant was ordering the impassive Spanish driver, in a stream of more and more abusive Spanish, to straighten his cart; but even as she watched, the Spaniard shrugged his huge shoulders and climbed down from the cart, pointedly handing his whip over to the furious lieutenant.

The crowd roared its appreciation of this jest. Since they outnumbered the French, they were using the opportunity to vent their feelings in a small way toward the hated occupiers.

A less strong-minded woman certainly would have withdrawn at that point. Reggie merely lifted her skirts from the filthy cobblestones and pushed her way through the crowd. She scorned to shirk unpleasantness when a little exertion on her part might avert a tragedy.

But even as she advanced, she saw the cart begin to topple and the child beneath. She was still too far away to do any more than shout a warning, which she knew had little chance of being heard in that voluble crowd.

Then, even as she watched in horror, she saw the tall peasant leap forward and snatch the child out of danger. He was clearly risking his own life to do it; but even then he might have made it had he not launched himself next, even as the overbalanced cart toppled, at the legs of a fat shopkeeper standing frozen in shock and seemingly unable to move.

The next moment, Reggie stood in helpless dread as the brave stranger was buried under a killing avalanche of heavy logs.

The major, aware only for an endless time of being battered and pummeled on all sides, had ample time to reflect bitterly on so ignominious an ending to his military career.

He fully expected to be killed, but luck was once more with him it seemed. When it was over he lay, only half conscious and unable to catch his breath, but almost miraculously alive.

How long he was likely to remain that way was another question. Even as painful reality began to intrude itself, a heavy log was hastily lifted off his chest and he found himself confronted by a party of anxious citizens, peering worriedly down at him. Battered and half-conscious as he was, it was only his well-honed instinct for danger that kept him from ruining himself right then. He knew he faced perhaps the worst scrape of his military career. While he might pass for a native for an hour or two, in casual meetings, he could never hope to keep up the masquerade for a longer time— especially if he were ill or out of his senses. And if he were not out of the town before the gates closed at dusk, the chances of his being discovered increased a hundredfold.

His rescuers, seemingly encouraged by not finding a lifeless corpse, immediately launched into a heated debate over his head about the best way to deal with the emergency. The stout shopkeeper he had flung out of danger, his own clothes torn and one cheek slightly grazed, was urging sensibly that he should be kept still while *el doctor* was sent for. A small farmer, smelling of garlic and onions, insisted as loudly that he should be carried to the nearest house where his injuries might be attended to; while a wizened grandmother in the rusty black of the Spanish peasant, taking in his extreme pallor and the blood upon his face, crossed herself piously and expressed the opinion that someone should run immediately to fetch the priest.

The major knew that any of the three would likely spell his ruin. He felt as if he had been trampled by a troop of cavalry—an unpleasant experience that had actually happened to him in battle once—but he tried to gather enough breath to assure them that he needed none of those. But his lungs seemed to be permanently deflated, and he could get out no more than a hoarse groan.

One motherly soul, taking up the farmer's recommendation, was loudly insisting that he should come home with her, the *pobrecito*, where she would soon have him well again. It was a crime, it was, how the despised French could endanger even the most innocent of citizens, and it was only thanks to the stranger's quick actions that they hadn't all been crushed to death where they stood.

She no doubt meant well, but all in all he could have done without her strident championship. So far the French soldiers were only looking bored by the mishap, but that could change at any moment.

He tried to take a quick inventory of his ills to see what he had to contend with. He suspected he had broken his collarbone, for he could feel the pieces of bone grating painfully together, and possibly his left arm, for it seemed to be more or less useless. He had probably broken some ribs as well, which explained the shortness of breath and the agonizing pain whenever he moved. As for the internal damage he had sustained under that murderous pummeling, he dared not think. His head also felt as if it were being hammered at from the inside, and seemed to be stuffed with cotton wool, making any cogent thought extremely difficult, and he became belatedly aware that there was blood trickling down his face.

But all in all, he knew he was lucky to be alive. His hands were scraped and raw, and he did not doubt the rest of his body had suffered similarly. In fact it seemed fair to predict that he would be black and blue all over by tomorrow—were he still alive by then and not in some French prison, which seemed more than probable. But at least none of his hurts were immediately fatal. He had broken his collarbone once before, in a fall from a horse, and knew that it was painful but not serious, and the rest were merely inconvenient.

But if he intended to remain alive, and not a French prisoner, it was clear he would soon somehow have to thank his well-wishers and get up and walk away under his own power, then make it to the gates of the town, and out the road for some two miles, where his horse was patiently cropping grass waiting for him.

He tried to dismiss the unwelcome suspicion that in his present state he might as well have been aiming for the moon.

By the time Reggie managed to reach him, she had somewhere lost all her parcels in her headlong push through the crowd, and her skirt had long since been allowed to drag into the mud, which would no doubt earn her Conchita's soft-voiced exclamations of reproach. But she was unaware of either of those unimportant details.

She had not expected to find the tall stranger alive, but as the logs were lifted off him, she saw that he was not only miraculously somehow still alive, but seemed to be conscious. Still she pushed through, for he had invited her admiration with his quick instincts and courage in saving the small boy; and she feared if the crowd was allowed to have its way he might yet be allowed to die of his wounds.

It was only as she drew near, that something, she hardly knew what, in his eyes, perhaps, or the way he held his head, had her halting again, at first in astonished disbelief, then in increasing horrified certainty. She had no idea what an Englishman was doing in Burgos, but she fought her way through the crowd toward him with suddenly much more than ordinary concern.

Adam, swearing under his breath at the unkind trick of fate that had placed him in so ludicrous and dangerous a position, was trying not to swoon away again. He knew he needed all his wits about him if he were to survive this disaster, and at the moment it was all he could do to fight against the waves of blackness that threatened to overcome him again.

It was then that the unexpected intervention occurred. A calm and well-bred feminine voice could be heard saying authoritatively over his head, in the purest Castilian Spanish, "Let me through. Pray let me through."

To his surprise the crowd respectfully parted. The next moment a slim figure in the rich black of the Spanish aristocrat, but without the enveloping mantilla, had reached him and was kneeling beside him, ignoring the mire in the road or his battered and bloodstained appearance. She took his hand in her own smooth, cool one and competently felt for his pulse, saying firmly, "Pray lie still sir, and don't try to talk. You shall be better presently."

He wondered incredulously if she could be a nurse, or even a nun; but her rich clothes and assured demeanor argued against either. He was well aware that aristocratic Spanish ladies did not go unescorted on the streets, especially young and pretty ones, as he took in vaguely that this one was. She was also much younger than her calm confidence would suggest, which puzzled him still further. But all in all, a rich Spaniard was likely to prove more dangerous to him than the peasants around him, and so he tried to mutter that he was all right, there was no need to bother.

The warm pressure on his hand seemed to increase strongly and he was betrayed into raising his eyes to her face once again. Her own eyes seemed to stare at him fixedly, which puzzled him still more, but even as he watched, her long dark lashes fell again and she said, still calmly and firmly, "Pray don't try to talk, sir. I will have you carried to my house, where your wounds can be attended to."

The odd pressure on his hand had increased. He cast another swift glance upward, and was further startled by a faint but unmistakable shake of her head.

Mystified, but acknowledging grimly that he was at the moment beyond the strength it would require to extricate himself from this newest and probably disastrous development, he obediently kept silent. At her command three stout peasants lifted him gingerly. She seemed remarkably self-possessed for so young a woman, but for the moment her

interference had at least had one positive effect. Most of his
well-wishers soon melted away once they saw him under
such obviously capable care, and the soldiers were thankfully still too preoccupied with righting the cart and clear-
ing the street, under the contemptuous jibes of the Spanish
onlookers, to pay much attention to what was happening.
Only the stout matron remained to volubly advise and su-
pervise the lifting of the patient.

The major, too battered and worn out to try and make
any further sense of the mystery, had all he could do to endure this operation without fainting dead away.

In fact, he soon discovered even that was a hopeless
goal. They tried to be careful in lifting him, but he was
soon gritting his teeth as he was clumsily raised, and clung
to his swimming senses only with an enormous effort of
will.

It was then, when he could no longer be certain his brain
was not playing some unlikely and ludicrous trick upon
him, that he thought he heard his rescuer say in his ear,
very softly and in English, "Don't worry. You are safe
enough. Just don't speak."

It was a piece of advice, at least, that was no longer necessary. By then he could not have spoken if he tried. The
next moment the pain had grown so exquisite that he was
almost grateful when the blackness at last overtook him.

Chapter 3

REGGIE WAS THANKFUL that he soon lapsed into unconsciousness as she had him carried to her house and up to a little-used room on the third floor. She dreaded to think what damage they might be doing in moving him, but that was of less consideration at the moment than the fear that he might mumble something in English at any moment and even yet give himself away.

The household servants were predictably horrified at the sight of their mistress accompanied by so dirty and blood-stained a stranger. These she hurriedly dispatched about their business, save for one sent flying to bring the old priest, who had some rudimentary knowledge of medicine and might be trusted to the last degree. Another she sent to fetch her sister's stout old nurse, who also might be relied upon to keep her mouth shut.

Maria, stout and phlegmatic, soon stumped heavily up the stairs. She cast one extremely shrewd glance at Reggie, busy cleaning the worst of the blood from the stranger's face, and then with a shrug she went wordlessly to help. Between them they managed to clean their patient up and tend to the more minor of his hurts, revealing as they did so a surprisingly comely profile and a noble form. This merely reinforced Reggie in her belief that he was no Spanish peasant, but Maria made no comment then, either. She merely cast another sharp glance at her mistress before stumping off to discard the bloodstained cloths.

Father Gregorio, when he came, also asked very few

questions. The broken collarbone he professed not to trouble him, nor yet the broken ribs, unless of course they had punctured the lung, which fortunately did not look to be the case. The many cuts and bruises were only to be expected, given the nature of the mishap, and indeed he expressed the opinion that their unknown patient must be under God's protection to have survived such an accident.

He looked more grave about the blow to the head and the prolonged faint, however, and frowned heavily over the left shoulder, fearing it was beyond his simple skill to mend. He had known cases where the shoulder, left unattended, had frozen and the arm was never after of any use—a sad fate for so brave a man.

"We will hope that is not the case, Father," Reggie said firmly, refusing to give in to so pessimistic a view.

"Of course, my child." The old priest was a deceptively simple man, growing frail and white-haired, but with a touching faith in his fellow man and a twinkling tolerance that Reggie had long found more than admirable. "But it is in God's hands, not ours."

Before she could speak again, he added calmly, "But you took a risk in bringing him here, my child. But that, too, I would say is in God's hands, not ours."

Reggie shot him a swift glance. She was not herself so inclined to trust in a benevolent fate, but she had purposely said nothing to the old priest about her suspicions, wanting to see if he, too, saw anything out of the ordinary. "Ah! Then you, too, think—?" She asked quickly.

"It is certain he is not Spanish," he answered, his serenity wholly unimpaired. "Nor would you have sent for me if he were merely who he appears to be."

"No. I wanted to see if you agreed with me."

"He has not spoken?"

"Only in Spanish. He fooled the crowd, at least."

Father Gregorio momentarily betrayed his aristocratic origins by being unimpressed by that. "But then that is easily done. To sustain such a masquerade as we suspect for a longer period—and under such circumstances—is a very different matter. God must indeed be protecting him, for it was fortunate you happened to be by when the incident occurred, my child."

Reggie tended to agree wholeheartedly with that, at least. "Nevertheless, if our suspicions *are* correct, you're right there is some danger in harboring him. I would understand if you didn't wish to become involved."

"My daughter, I am far too old to fear any but heavenly punishment," the old priest told her simply. "And I know you too well by now to fear that danger will deter you. As I said, he is a most fortunate man. God must indeed be with him."

Stout Maria had remained silent throughout this exchange, but now she automatically crossed herself, though her next words somewhat belied the pious gesture. "Hmmph! It seems to me we are all in need of His mercies at the moment," she said bluntly. "I do not complain—in this house it would do little good if I did!—but it occurs to me you are both mad. But then I have long resigned myself to that. But perhaps you will tell me what am I to say to the rest of those lazy pigs belowstairs when they ask why Señorita Reggie has brought home this wounded stranger, and none but myself is allowed to attend him?"

"Tell them he saved a boy in the marketplace from being crushed to death," said Reggie quickly. "They will hear of it soon enough, I imagine. If they are still curious, tell them it is but another of my foreign whims. They all think me mad anyway."

"Hmmph!" said Maria again, not disputing it. "And if word should reach Don Ottavio's ears? Not even for the good priest here will I have him upset."

"I will myself call upon him when we are finished here, and casually mention the presence of the poor wounded boy," said the ancient priest calmly. "At any rate, you have nothing to fear, my daughter. He may be frail in body, but his spirit has not failed him. He would never close his doors to one who fights to rescue our poor country from the French."

The nurse shrugged and said no more, and in the end the priest merely bound the shoulder tightly, trusting to God's will and the healing properties of rest. Between them, he and Maria then sent Reggie firmly out of the room while the few remaining tattered garments were stripped from their patient and he was put into one of her stepbrother Filipe's nightshirts.

Reggie accepted this banishment meekly, although she had by then seen enough to know the stranger was loose-limbed and surprisingly well muscled. Nor would her own modesty have stopped short at stripping him herself if it had proven necessary. She had not experienced the least faintness when his fairly unpleasant wounds were laid bare, and knew herself to be thankfully deficient in the more feminine weaknesses.

Her patient was at least conscious when she visited him later. He was looking slightly better though still alarmingly pale and in obvious pain. But it was possible to gain some hint at least of what he must look like under normal circumstances. And she had been right that he was a decidedly attractive man. His skin and hair were both dark, no doubt allowing him to pass for a Spaniard when necessary, but his eyes were a somewhat startling blue. There were also attractive ridges cut in his lean cheeks, as if he smiled often, and the hint of lines at the corners of his eyes, as if he spent a good deal of time squinting into the sun. All in all she liked what she saw, and so came on into the room, her own eyes twinkling a little.

He was regarding her in some puzzlement, a heavy frown between his brows, and had stiffened as she entered, as if braced for something. She guessed that he was feeling both battered and more than worried, and so she said quickly, and in English, "My dear sir, you are perfectly safe, I promise you. How are you feeling?"

The frown was still very much in place, but the puzzle-

ment had only increased. "Good God, you *are* English!" he
exclaimed weakly, and in the same language. "I thought
surely I must have dreamt it. But how—why—? It was you
in the street who rescued me? But how did you guess—?"

"That you were English?" she asked matter-of-factly.
"You did not give yourself away, if that is what you fear. In
fact, at first I meant only to rescue you from the well-mean-
ing attentions of the crowd, which seemed to me likely to
ensure your death if the accident had not already done so.
But then something—I hardly know what—made me suspect the truth. No one else suspected anything, though, I
would stake my life on that."

"You may well have to." His weak voice sounded unexpectedly grim. "And you had me brought here? My dear
girl—" Words seemed to fail him, and he looked indeed so
ill that she went quickly to measure out the dose Father
Gregorio had left for him.

"Yes, but all that is better left for tomorrow," she said
cheerfully. "For the moment you have nothing to do but get
better. Now here is a probably foul-tasting medicine I am to
see you drink."

He would have protested, but she gave him no opportunity. She expertly raised his head and ruthlessly tilted the
draft down his throat. He drank, willy-nilly, choking a little, and when she lowered his head again, he was so clearly
exhausted he could only lie with his eyes closed, that
alarming pallor more marked than ever on his face.

She waited until she was sure he was asleep then tiptoed
quietly from the room.

She checked on him several times during the night,
ghostly in her nightrail and with only a candle to light her,
but each time he seemed to be breathing normally and in a
deep sleep. Once he muttered something, which she could
not catch, and another time she had to replace the covers he
had thrown off in some restlessness. But he did not speak
again, or betray any sign of consciousness.

She was there again, fully dressed, at an early hour of the morning, this time the stout Maria in her wake.

He, too, was awake, and looking encouragingly stronger. By then he needed a shave, and his bruises had come out in all their glory, making him look like some parti-colored clown. But his eyes were brighter, and he had lost a good deal of the pain-glazed look he had worn the day before.

"Good," she said cheerfully, coming into the room and gesturing Maria to put down the tray she carried. "You are looking much better this morning."

"I am," said her patient, even his voice sounding stronger. "But I must tell you, ma'am, I became convinced in the watches of the night that I had only dreamt you. In fact, you are clearly nothing but a figment of my imagination, and I suspect I will shortly wake up to discover I am even now in a French prison."

She laughed. "Oh, I am real enough, I assure you. But I don't wonder at your astonishment." She calmly moved to take his pulse and was relieved to discover that though his skin felt a little feverish under her fingers, it was much stronger than the day before. "I think the fates must be determined to protect you, my dear sir, for it was only the merest chance that took me that particular way yesterday morning."

"I begin to think you must be right." His voice was still weak, but unmistakably educated, and made her think instantly of her father. It was a shock to realize how long it had been since she had heard English spoken. "I am immensely grateful, that goes without saying. But you should not have had me brought here."

"We can worry about that later. It seemed to me of first importance to remove you from the vicinity of those French soldiers. And you are perfectly safe here, I promise you."

"Good God, that is not what I fear!" The deep frown was between his eyes again. "It is your safety I am concerned about."

"My dear sir, you are worrying over a trifle. There is

very little risk, I promise you. It is unfortunate that your—mishap—was quite so public, for you have become something of a hero, I fear, and it is bound to be talked of in the town. But I shall take care to nurse you myself, aided only by one of the servants who is completely to be trusted. Under the circumstances I dared not call in a physician, so the local priest bound up your wounds and did what he could for you. But you may trust him with your life, for he would never betray you. The other servants in the house know only that you are a wounded stranger, and since they shall not be allowed near you, you have nothing to fear."

He closed his eyes wearily, as if finding it more than he could cope with at the moment. "I can only repeat, it is not for myself I fear. But if I were to be discovered here, you and your entire household would be in jeopardy. Surely you know that? I must be out of here at once."

"Yes, yes, we can talk of all that later," she said soothingly. "Now I have another noxious draft to give you, and then I will leave you in peace."

Ill as he was, he seemed to find her determined cheerfulness somewhat trying. "My dear foolish child—!" he bit out, then he shook his head as if to clear it and passed a weak hand over his eyes. "I beg your pardon. You are an angel of mercy, and you undoubtedly saved my life, for which I must be eternally grateful. If only I could *think*!"

"Well, since it is a miracle you are alive at all, and you no doubt have a pounding headache, besides feeling as if you had been pummeled all over, it is scarcely surprising you cannot think," she told him sensibly, expertly measuring out the potion Father Gregorio had left her.

That seemed to exasperate him still more. "Do you think I am a child to be cajoled out of a bad temper?" he demanded in weak frustration. "I tell you—"

"Tell me another time. Now you are in pain and will do very much better to leave it all until you are feeling more yourself. And if you do not wish to be mistaken for a child,

mind you don't behave like one, and drink your medicine
like a good boy."

"Damn it, girl—!"

As before, she gave him no chance to resist, but ruthlessly tilted the draft down his throat. Though he again was
obliged to swallow it, she was to discover he had recovered
more strength than she had expected. His good hand
reached out to grasp her wrist, and when she would have
moved away his grasp tightened with unexpected force.
"This time, I am not to be fobbed off so easily," he said
grimly. "More is at stake than I think you can know. And I
can't risk your being associated with me."

"My dear sir," she said calmly, "it has been quite clear to
me from the beginning that you are an English spy. Why
else do you think I rescued you?"

Chapter 4

HIS HAND TIGHTENED alarmingly on her wrist.

She obediently remained still under his grip, but the look she slanted down at him held amusement, and something else. "I can only repeat, you are worried over nothing, you know. There is very little danger."

The major, battered and weak and coping with a pounding head, belatedly realized what he was doing and released her wrist, then passed his hand over his eyes, feeling more and more as if he had stumbled into a dream. His remarkable rescuer was that morning dressed in a pale, becoming muslin, and looked cool and composed, as if she rescued wounded spies every morning of the week. Her sangfroid, indeed, wholly belied her age, which he guessed to be no more than two-and-twenty. But he began to see why, in his first dazed reaction, he had wondered if she was a nurse, or even a nun.

He also saw why he had at first mistaken her for a Spaniard, for like himself her hair was a rich, vivid brown, dressed at the moment in a simple style that became her; her skin was creamy pale, and her eyes, which were particularly well spaced and fine, a dark brown. But on second glance it was hard to believe her anything but English, for she seemed to be wholly without the shy modesty that marked the well-brought-up Spanish girl.

Nor was she by any means a traditional beauty. Her face was too lively and decided for that. Intelligence and considerable humor shone out of her wide eyes—her only real claim to beauty—and her mouth was large and mobile, while her nose and chin both betrayed considerable strength of purpose, if not outright stubbornness. Aside from those obvious attributes, she revealed a slim and elegant figure and particularly beautiful hands, as well as a self-possession that would have befitted a woman twice her age.

In fact she seemed so much in command of the situation that his eyes went instinctively to her hands again, searching for a wedding ring. It occurred to him she must be a young matron, perhaps married to some Spanish grandee, which would at least explain the mystery that had been occupying him since he had wakened at an early hour, too sore to go back to sleep.

But her slim fingers revealed no ring of any sort to explain her remarkable calm. He was conscious of an absurd sense of relief out of proportion to its cause.

With an effort he pulled himself together, wondering how he could make her realize the danger, if she did not already. What she was doing there, and how she had happened to be handy to rescue him were puzzles that only added to the unreality of the present situation, and he was, in addition, having to fight the impulse just to close his eyes again and drift, letting this remarkable girl take care of things as she seemed perfectly willing to do.

But he knew that way lay disaster, and so he made himself say weakly, "My dear child, I confess I understand none of it—especially how I should contrive to be rescued by the only known Englishwoman in all of northern Spain."

She laughed at that. "Yes, Father Gregorio—he's the priest who dressed your wounds—thinks God must indeed be watching over you."

"Or else it is a case of the devil taking care of his own. What on earth are you doing living here in a French-occupied town?"

She calmly seated herself in a chair by the bedside. "Well, I will tell you, but only if you promise to drink up your soup, and to tell me at once if I am overtiring you."

He saw that the maid with her had brought a covered tray, which she now uncovered to reveal a bowl of steaming soup and a pitcher and glass. She had as yet said nothing, but now she set down the tray, muttered something under her breath in Spanish, and stalked out.

He was well aware that the more people to know of his presence the more danger he—and his unknown rescuer—were in. But the present situation was already so outside his control that it seemed pointless to make an objection. He discovered instead that he was very thirsty, if not particularly hungry, but he said with some exasperation, "My dear ma'am, you seem to persist in believing me a recalcitrant schoolboy, to be cajoled into doing what he is bid."

"Yes, but in my experience all men revert to schoolboys whenever they are ill," she retorted frankly, taking up a spoon. "Be they never so advanced in years and wisdom, they discard all common sense and expect to be made instantly well again, while being wholly impatient with anything that might make them so!"

"You are too severe, ma'am. But you are certainly not going to feed me, if that is what you have in mind," he objected strongly, forgetting larger issues for the moment. "I still have the use of my right hand, you know."

"Ah, but I should perhaps have warned you from the beginning that I am a confirmed autocrat, my dear sir. You will get not one word of my story out of me until you agree to behave sensibly. Now open your mouth like a good boy."

He was torn between weak amusement and annoyance at her dictatorial manner, but after a short struggle with himself he meekly opened his mouth and swallowed the soup she proffered. "I begin to think you are indeed an autocrat, ma'am," he agreed weakly. "But fair is fair. You were about to tell me your story."

"Well, I warn you it is a long one and will probably leave you feeling more feverish than you are already." She duly presented another spoonful of her broth. "I was indeed born in England, but I confess I have not set foot in that country for a great number of years. My father was Sir Francis Alderstock, of the Diplomatic Corps and I have spent far more time abroad than in England in my lifetime. I have lived in Madrid, Rome, Lisbon, and even Paris. I speak French, Spanish, Portuguese, and Italian fluently, and can get by in German if I have to."

"Most impressive," he murmured, again obediently swallowing a spoonful of her soup. It seemed easier to do as he was bid than argue with her.

She laughed and shook her head. "On the contrary, it should be wonderful indeed if I did not speak those languages. I told you I've spent far more time abroad than at home. Anyway, my father's last posting was in Madrid."

"His last?" he repeated. His head still felt a little as if someone were beating with a hammer inside his skull, and his brain was annoyingly fuzzy, but he did not miss the past tense. "He's dead?"

"Yes. He died there, nearly eight years ago."

The length of time surprised him. "And you did not return home then?"

For the first time she seemed to hesitate. "I daresay it is hard to explain," she admitted, presenting another spoonful of her soup, "but we had been in England so very little in our lives—Mama and I—that it scarcely felt like home to either of us any longer. Add to that the fact that my mother was raised in the old school, for Papa had made *all* the decisions, you see. She relied upon him completely, so that she was really at a loss when he died, poor dear. Unfortunately I was as yet too young to be much help to her, I'm sorry to say, and all in all it was a very difficult time. We meant to go home, of course, but the only relations we had in England anymore were my paternal grandparents, whom Mama had never gotten along with. I loved my mother dearly, you must understand, but she was *not* strong and required someone to—to support her spirits, which I fear my grandparents would never have done. Oh dear, I knew this would better be left to when you are feeling a little stronger. I suspect I should not be addling your brains with such nonsense."

He shook his head. "You are not addling my brains." He was also beginning to get her measure by then, and added, "And so I take it you decided it would be better to marry your mother off to a Spaniard rather than subject her to your grandparents' bracing indifference?"

She looked up, quick amusement lighting her face in a way that corrected him in his first impression that she was not a beauty. "I can see I shall have to take care around you! You are far too clever by half, especially for a seriously wounded man. I can also see you have already guessed that I did *not* inherit my mother's yielding disposition. But yes, I must confess it seemed to me, all in all, that she would be made very unhappy in England, declining into a mere widow, and having to endure that cold, damp climate after so many years abroad. Fortunately, Don Ottavio had always been a strong admirer of hers, for she was just the sort of pretty, yielding female inclined to appeal to Spanish gallantry—unlike her far-from-yielding daughter, I regret to say! At any rate, he proposed, and I must confess it seemed to me to be the perfect answer. And before you say anything more, let me assure you I did nothing to force him into the match, for he was most sincerely attached to her, I promise you. And so she married him, and all in all it worked out very well."

He had overtaxed his weak strength and was beginning to long for the comforting oblivion of sleep again, but he liked her lively sense of humor, and so he murmured, trying to ease his aching head a little, "You are to be congratulated." He discovered without much surprise that the new position was just as bad as the old one.

"Ah, you obviously mistake me for one of those horrible, managing females," she told him in amusement, moving to adjust his pillow for him in a way that somehow managed to be a thousand times more comfortable. "There, is that better? I will readily confess that I am, like most inveterate meddlers, usually convinced most people would be better off if only they would follow my advice. But I promise you in this case I was right. Mama could not have abided being surrounded by complaining and disapproving relations and having to look after herself, for she was so pretty and fragile and so easily cast down by—by oppressive spirits. That is yet another thing I did not inherit from her, by the way! I fear I take after my poor papa. But anyway, the marriage answered excellently, as I said. Don Ottavio practically doted upon her, and even his children came to love her, and we went on famously for a number of years. Even when—even when the French invaded, it seemed—well, I daresay you can scarcely understand it, but Don Ottavio was in fragile health by then, and there seemed no thought of taking him to England, and besides, we both had come to think of Spain as our home by then. And everyone hoped, of course, that it would not be for very long. I only wish—"

When she hesitated, he said gently, "Forgive me, but I gather your mother is dead as well, now?"

She blinked rapidly, but quickly recovered from what he by now recognized as an uncharacteristic show of weakness. "Yes, which is why I was so particularly pleased her last years were happy ones. She died over a year ago, and I don't think she ever regretted not returning to England."

He lay silently for a moment, taking it all in. "And yet you still did not return yourself?" It seemed incredible to him.

She shrugged. "It must seem odd, I know," she confessed lightly, offering another spoonful of her broth. "And I considered going home, of course, except that really I had nowhere to go by then, for even my grandparents were dead. And my family here has been so kind to me, and being the managing female I am, I will confess I am not at all sure they could get along without me. So here I remain, and that is more than enough for now. I fear I have already talked you into a fever. It is time I let you rest again."

"No, don't go yet." When her brows rose at his dictatorial tone, he countered more meekly, "Please. You have entertained me most pleasantly, but now tell me what you have so plainly been skirting around since you came. How badly am I injured?"

"I have been hiding nothing, I promise you. According to Father Gregorio you have a mild concussion, a body covered in scrapes and bruises, and several cracked ribs."

He groaned. "Yes, that damnable cart! I beg your pardon. What else? I seem to remember my collarbone felt broken."

She sobered. "Yes, but Father Gregorio assures me that is relatively minor." She hesitated, then added as if unwillingly, "It is your shoulder that is the more serious, if you must know, for he fears it is broken as well. We dared not bring a doctor to you, for though the Spanish hate the French well enough, we were not sure many would risk their lives to protect you. But Father Gregorio believes that it will heal in time."

He passed over that. "I have had broken bones before," he said impatiently. "They don't trouble me. What else?"

"Well, you have the devil's own headache, of course, but I suspect I needn't tell you that. There is always a risk, according to Father Gregorio, that concussions can be serious, but you would seem to have all your faculties about you, so I am not worried. And now I have exhausted you enough with my prattle."

He decided, even in his present exhausted and battered state, that he liked the way her eyes twinkled when she was amused, but he was still pursuing his own thoughts. A sharp frown remained between his brows as he demanded absently, "By the by, who undressed me yesterday?"

Her eyes broke into outright laughter. "Ah, I should have suspected so much meekness! Did you think to put me to the blush, my dear sir?"

He was startled, for his mind had been elsewhere. "No, on my honor! That would indeed be churlish."

"And futile as well," she assured him. "I fear I am shockingly lacking in the feminine sensibilities and in a pinch would not have hesitated to strip you myself. But fortunately my maidenly modesty was preserved, for Father Gregorio and María possess all the decorum I fear I so sadly lack, and banished me from the room while you were made comfortable. But I warn you now I shall change your bandages without a moment's hesitation and even shave you in a few days."

"That at least I shall be spared," he informed her strongly. "Grateful as I am to you, Miss Alderstock, you must see I cannot stay here. I am putting your whole household at risk."

"My dear sir, we have plucked that crow already. It will be time enough to discuss it when you are strong enough to sit up for half an hour without feeling as weak as a kitten, as you do now. Don't think it has escaped me that for all your bravado you are knocked into cinders, and little wonder. You are extremely lucky to be alive. Now try to get some sleep, and I will be back again this evening, if not sooner."

He stared up at her impotently. He had little experience and still less liking of playing the invalid, but he had already been forced to acknowledge that he would accomplish little but his own capture by insisting upon leaving now. The importance of his mission, and the risk of involving her in danger fretted at him, nor did it help to find himself treated as a slightly retarded child by this odd girl. It was a situation all the more ludicrous since he guessed he could easily give her a dozen years.

But he discovered, as before, that her vile-tasting potion, which undoubtedly contained a sleeping draft of some kind, was already taking effect, for he was finding it increasingly hard to keep his eyes open.

It was only when he had all but lost the battle that he realized that he still knew nothing but the last name of his somewhat extraordinary benefactress. It suddenly seemed to him of immense importance to know what her first name was, but he fell asleep before he could ask her.

Chapter 5

THE NEXT TIME she returned she was again not alone. It was dusk, and she carried a tray while a shorter and younger figure bore a lighted lantern.

All in all, it already seemed as if a disastrous number of people knew of his presence in the house, but the major was hardly in a position to protest. He saw that they were both in evening dress, Miss Alderstock in a deep crimson that became her admirably, and the newcomer, a decidedly pretty girl, in the traditional black of the well-born Spanish señorita, and he realized it must be near to dinnertime.

Even so, he was glad enough of the interruption. He had been lying there for some time, all too aware of discomfort in so many parts of his body he could not distinguish them all—a pain which rose to active agony whenever he moved or tried to find a more comfortable spot.

And his physical ills were far less troublesome than his mental ones. His head still felt as if it would break in two with any unwise movement on his part, and it was unfortunately at a time when he had never needed all his wits about him more. It was clearly of the utmost importance he get his message through, and at the same time he faced the unwelcome truth that the longer he remained there, tied so painfully by the heels, the more he was putting the whole household in danger. Those two inexorable facts beat at his brain, adding further to his headache, for he could see no clear way, at the moment, of solving either of them.

He was therefore glad of any distraction and relieved to

see his comely young rescuer again. He had been tended earlier in the day by the stout and forbidding Spanish nurse, who had glowered and seen to his needs with scant gentleness.

As if reading his mind, Miss Alderstock said cheerfully, "You are awake, then. And looking as blue as megrim, as well, I see. My dear sir, have you been lying there uselessly fretting yourself into a fever?"

"If I look blue, which I don't doubt for a moment, you must blame it on my present battered state," he countered weakly. "I promise you I am more than delighted to see you."

"If only to relieve the boredom?" she teased him. "But I have brought you another visitor as well, as you see. And I hope you are hungry again, for here is some more soup. You will be relieved to hear, however, that I don't propose to feed you this time. I think between us we can contrive to raise you on your pillows so that you can feed yourself, and thus protect your injured dignity."

"Thank you. But neither you nor your sister are to be waiting upon me," he said firmly. "I am delighted with your visit, but I would far prefer you left me to the tender mercies of the rather remarkable female that was here earlier."

She laughed. "Oh, Maria has a gruff exterior, but a heart of gold, I promise you. She was my stepsister's old nurse, and rules us all with a rod of iron. As for our nursing you, you must know my stepfather is in very frail health, and we are both of us more than accustomed to the sickroom."

"But hardly in your best gowns. In fact, I suspect you are going out this evening, and I beg you will not alter your plans for my sake."

"No, indeed we are not going out. You must know we live a very quiet life just at present. If fact, we merely hoped to impress you with our finery." She swept a hand to include their dresses, which were of the very latest fashion. "There is at least one advantage to a French occupation, you know, for the latest in French fashions are always easily obtainable."

Before he quite realized it, or could object, she had adroitly lifted his head and shoulders and her sister had whisked two more pillows beneath him, so that when she laid him gently back again he was halfway sitting up.

He had no choice but to endure their ministrations, though he was feeling annoyingly ill by the end of it, and could only mentally swear again at his own weakness. "I am duly impressed," he managed breathlessly, "but I fear you are wasting such refinements on me, my dear ma'am. The last ball I attended most of the ladies wore darned mantillas and three-year-old gowns, and we officers had to draw straws to see which of us would stay home in order to provide a complete dress uniform for the lucky ones."

She laughed and arranged the tray across his lap. "Ah, well. In that case I will confess we had another reason as well. We are expecting visitors later, which is why we came so early. A very distinguished visitor, as a matter of fact. The French commandant of the town."

She handed him the spoon as she spoke, but he had already stiffened instinctively. He had no idea how he must have looked until her sister protested in gentle, accented English, "Reggie! *Nombre de Dios,* it is not kind to alarm our poor patient so!"

"Yes, so I see," she said with interest. "My dear sir, you looked quite murderous there for a moment, even in your present weakened state. Did you think I meant to turn you in to claim the reward? There is one, you know. For anyone turning in or informing on any English soldier. If the French can't win our loyalty, they mean to try to buy it instead."

He relaxed again slowly and took up the spoon, concentrating on feeding himself without any humiliating spills. "Forgive me. Only for a moment," he said truthfully. "But at least I have one question answered that has been puzzling me."

It was her turn to look mystified. "Indeed? And what is that?"

"Your name. I have spent the day, when I was not dozing from that wretched potion you gave me or enduring the ministrations of your sister's nurse, speculating on what it might be. Clearly nothing traditional, like Jane or Anne would suit you, nor even the more romantic ones, like Clorinda or Ariel. But Reggie! Yes, I like it. Unusual and refreshing."

"Well, I hope you did not really waste your day on such an absurd pursuit as that," she told him in amusement. "But you must think me a complete shatter-brain! I am Regina Alderstock—called Reggie by my friends and family, as you have already seen. Regina smacks far too much of a royal dignity I all too wholly lack. And this is my sister, Dona Concepcion Luisa Margaretta de los Angeles y Vanegas, a name that suits her far better than mine does, I think you will agree. But being the infidel Englishwoman I am, I call her Conchita."

Her sister blushed and protested. She was a very pretty girl of nineteen or so, with all the shyness and demure gentleness her stepsister so markedly lacked. "And that suits me very well," she said in her soft, accented English. "But I fear we must hurry, dearest Reggie, for it would never do to make Monsieur de Thierry suspicious."

"No, indeed," Reggie agreed. "But it has occurred to me, confirmed shatter-brain that I am, that we don't know the name of our guest, either. This is Spain, remember, and the proprieties must always be observed."

She turned expectant eyes to him, and he grinned weakly at her. "Perhaps not all the proprieties, for I fear I cannot make you a suitable bow just at this moment, but I am Major Adam Canfield, of the 7th Hussars, very much at your service, as I think you know."

"Ah, the amenities now being attended to," said Reggie cheerfully, "you may return to your soup."

"In a moment." He spoke again with that hint of authority that now and then betrayed him. "I confess I am curious. If you don't mean to turn me in, why have you invited the French commandant to call?"

"My dear Major, we haven't *invited* him. But one doesn't, if one is wise, offend the man responsible for the allocation of supplies and signing of passports to travel. And I confess he has proven useful on occasion."

"He has fallen in love with Reggie," supplied Conchita calmly.

"No such thing! He admires the liveliness of my mind! It seems the French like a little piquancy to counter all the Spanish gentleness and well-bred formality. You cannot know how set up in my own conceit that has made me, my dear Major, for in general, you know, no man looks twice at me after having seen my lovely sister."

"Reggie!" protested that damsel, blushing becomingly.

The major was looking between them with interest, but said merely, "He must know you're English, surely?"

"Oh, yes. But the French, however much I may despise their politics at the moment, are amazingly civilized, you know. And I am being unkind, for Monsieur de Thierry has been more than generous to us. I daresay it is absurd to blame him for the policies of his emperor, even as it would be absurd to blame poor Conchita here for the backbiting and machinations of the Spanish Court, or me for the complaining of Parliament."

"Don't I know it," he agreed feelingly. "We are often on far better terms with the French than we are with our own Cabinet, which sometimes seems to deliberately sabotage and annoy us. The troops, you know, often exchange pleasantries. Our pickets have been known to object when they see the French are setting their own pickets too close, for it means a night of useless alarums; and the French as often as not take their advice. And there have been times when the troops leave out a few coins and a bowl, and will find it filled with brandy the next morning. Only I can tell you they were pretty hot the morning they found their coins gone and the bowl empty."

"Oh, good, then you do understand," she said warmly. "And I should love to hear more of your adventures, when you are feeling rather better. But Conchita is right. We haven't much time, now, and you are still too battered to want to entertain us. She came because I thought it was time you made her acquaintance, in case she is required to deputize for me, and because I could not manage the tray and the lamp at the same time. But she means to visit her father before dinner, who is indeed bedridden most of the time now as I told you, and so must go now."

Conchita made her shy goodbyes, and slipped out, and Reggie turned to her patient then with her usual lack of self-consciousness, straightening his bedclothes and checking his bandages.

"But is it true the French commandant is in love with you?" he asked, frowning as he clumsily managed to raise another spoonful of thin broth to his mouth.

"No, no, that was just one of Conchita's jokes. We hold very sensible conversations on art and literature, I assure you, and there is not a hint of impropriety. He is a most cultured man, and very much married besides. He has a wife, I believe, back in Arles, and a quiverful of children. Conchita is so tenderhearted that it upsets her I have so few suitors to my name. All the men who come to the house fall instantly at her feet because she is so beautiful. Besides, most Spanish gentlemen do not care for my independence, I fear," she said with mock regret. "I am a decided oddity to them. They prefer their women to be shy and retiring, like Conchita, and I was never that, God knows. Even in my salad days."

He was still watching her with interest. He had abandoned the last of the soup and had collapsed gratefully back onto his pillows. "I don't believe a word of it," he said frankly now. "I have no great respect for the Spanish, but they cannot all be blind as well as foolish. Or did you merely make up that farrago of nonsense in order to get me to drink my soup?"

She laughed. "No, I am not so Machiavellian as that. It is true, I promise you. But if you want the whole truth I have discovered *they* are too dictatorial for me. How is that for turning an unpalatable truth into a virtue? I love my stepfather dearly, but I saw early on he would never have done as a husband for me. And since I am quite definitely on the shelf by now, for Spanish men, in general you know, desire very young wives, it is fortunate indeed that I am quite content with my lot. I could never hope to compete with Conchita. There, you have finished most of it like a good boy."

"My dear girl, it seems useless to point out to you that I am not a child," he murmured resignedly, his eyes wearily closed. "Or that I could easily give you a dozen years. But it might surprise you to learn a great many men prefer your style of beauty to hers. Pretty as she is, you have a certain sort of something that she lacks."

"And what might that be?" she asked, cocking her head and eyeing him quizzically, indeed as if she were humoring a child.

"Now I suspect you think to put me out of countenance!" he retorted weakly. "But you will not succeed. You must know you have a spirit, a charm, if you will, that she is wholly lacking."

"Oh, have I indeed? And that is precisely the sort of compliment men pay to girls who are not beauties, while themselves marrying the most beautiful girl they can find," she countered. "And this is an absurd conversation."

"I agree. And don't make me laugh," he begged. "It hurts too much. But without wishing to appear in the least uncomplimentary to your sister, I myself have a decided preference for your sort of looks."

"But then you are feeling grateful to me, and so could scarcely say anything else," she pointed out in amusement. "And I know now you must be recovering if you can pay me compliments, even absurd ones. I have carefully not inquired how you are doing, for I can see you are still pale and in a good deal of pain. Father Gregorio was half afraid one of your ribs might have punctured a lung, but I think now that cannot have been the case, thank goodness. And there are always worries after a blow to the head. I know you well enough by now to see that you mean to be stoical, but tell me *one* time how you are feeling, and I will not ask again tonight."

"Oh, I am doing very well, save a headache and general soreness."

"Yes, I should have known it was useless to ask you," she retorted. "You looked more dead than alive when we brought you here, and you are plainly still in a good deal of pain. But at least I hope you would tell me if you saw any cause for alarm. Then, risk or no risk, I must somehow contrive to get a doctor in to you. And I believe I know just the one. He is most reliable, and despises the French because his son was killed by them. I believe he might be trusted, though I didn't like to involve him unless it became absolutely necessary."

"Good God, no!" he said. "I have had broken bones before!"

"Yes, and mean to be stoical, which seems to me absurd," she said frankly. "Swear out loud if you feel like it. I won't mind. I have even been known to swear myself on occasion."

He smiled up at her, liking her very much, and said quietly, "Has anyone ever told you that you are a darling, Miss Regina Alderstock? But delightful as all this is, and grateful as I am to you, I can no longer afford to waste time on such absurdities, as you rightly call them. I have been lying here trying to think what is best to do, and I confess I cannot. But every hour I am here puts you and your family in more danger."

Her color had risen a little at his words, belying her boast that she was past blushing, but she said stoutly, "That it does not. And even if it did, we none of us—Conchita or

Don Ottavio or myself—would regard it, I promise you. They are true Spanish patriots, of whom there are more than you probably realize. I can only repeat that you are safe here for the moment. None of the servants save Maria has any inkling you are not what you appeared. I would advise you to concentrate on getting better and stop troubling yourself with fears that are wholly groundless and will only serve to keep your head in a worse whirl than it is already."

"It seems I have little choice in the matter at the moment," he admitted unwillingly. "But I must confess there is more at stake than even your safety. I notice you have been careful to ask me no questions, which proves to me that you are indeed a woman in a thousand. But since I have formed considerable respect for your intellect by now, I have no doubt you have guessed something of my mission. And it must be clear to you that aside from every other consideration, I cannot afford to be laid up here for more than a few days. I must get the information through that I was sent to collect."

"Yes, but I think I have a possible answer for you," she returned calmly. "I know of someone who might be able to get your message through safely in your stead."

"You are very kind. In fact, you have done far more than I have any right to expect already, but that is my problem," he said a little impatiently. "Anyway, we have tried using Spaniards before, and they either inflate the numbers of the enemy out of alarm, or underestimate them, thinking to please us. But in either case the result can be disastrous."

She laughed ruefully. "Oh dear! Yes, I love them dearly, but they are generally far too eager to please to be wholly reliable. I have had strangers on the street assure me that whatever house I am searching for is just ahead, out of a desire to reassure me, knowing all the while it is in quite the opposite direction. I must confess my English birth has prevailed there, for it has always seemed to me nonsensical. You ask a servant if a certain task has been done, and they invariably assure you it has, for they *mean* to get to it that day, or perhaps the next, and to them that is as good as if it had already been done. It is the one thing I have had the most difficulty in adjusting myself to."

"I can readily believe it," he agreed wearily. "I know Wellington grew sick enough of Spanish promises to deliver troops that never appeared, or more often, supplies that didn't even exist, to swear he would never deal with the Spanish generals again if he could help it. We never rely on their troops in battle, without a good number of our own officers among them, for though they are brave enough, they have no resolution and their officers are not trained in quick decisions or indeed in any decisions at all. They are good enough people, I daresay, but very bad soldiers."

"Yes, I can see they would be. They are taught the strictest obedience from infancy, you know, to both the Church and their fathers. Even Conchita is astonishingly docile and would not dream of contradicting her father, though to my mind he is by no means always right." Then she seemed to be amused at her own words. "Well, you must know by now that I myself do *not* take at all well to obedience of any kind. Nor was I reared to believe age automatically conferred infallible wisdom. But all this is very much beside the point. I was not suggesting a Spaniard should take your message for you."

"Then who?" He was merely humoring her and had not very much interest in her answer.

But in that he was mistaken, for she managed to surprise him yet again.

"Myself," she said simply. "Who else?"

Chapter 6

THAT JERKED HIM alert again and made him sit up so suddenly he winced. *"You?"* he repeated, dumbfounded.

"Yes, me," she returned calmly. "I don't mean to boast, but I am more reliable than the Spanish, and I suspect in a far better position than you to escape detection. Recollect that I am a familiar figure to the French, and have achieved the reputation of being something of an eccentric. I am quite accustomed to riding out on my own, for I have never adjusted myself to the Spanish notions of a duenna; moreover, I am known to be a friend to the local commandant. You see, it is the only logical solution."

"No!" he said explosively. "Far from being the only logical solution, it is completely out of the question! I won't even consider it!"

"Ah, but perhaps I should tell you that for some years I have been a go-between for the *guerrilleros*," she told him blithely. "My stepbrother, Filipe, though he is supposed to be in University at Madrid, is in reality with Julian Sanchez. I hope you don't question their efforts as much as you do the Spanish army?"

"No," he conceded unwillingly, frowning at her. "They have often proven invaluable at harrying the enemy's back, and keeping a constant pressure on them. But it is still out of the question. My dear girl, you may be every sort of a heroine—in fact, I am beginning to think you are!—but this is something very different. You would have to travel through the French lines even to reach the British army, and the journey would take you the better part of a week, without even considering the danger. The main part of our forces is somewhere south of Salamanca at present, and I know what the way is like. You could not possibly travel all that way alone. No, I tell you it is completely out of the question. I shall be fit enough in a few days."

"Dear me," she said, her eyes beginning to twinkle again. "I would never have suspected you of being so conventional."

That stung. "It is one thing to be conventional, quite another to be practical!" he snapped.

"Why, I would agree with you, for it is far more practical that I should make such a difficult journey than that you should undertake it in your present state. You won't be able to ride again for at least a fortnight."

"Not as much! Good God, I will be fit again in a day or two," he said impatiently.

"That you will not. It is a miracle you are alive. But, tell me, are you really willing to jeopardize your mission for the sake of your male pride? Even assuming you could get yourself onto a horse, you could never hope to get past the French guards, let alone all that way. And I shall not go alone, I assure you. That would be most improper!" Her eyes were quizzing him. "I shall be accompanied with the utmost decorum by my Spanish duenna and my younger sister. You must know we have been contemplating a journey to Salamanca for some while, for Conchita has an aunt there who is in ill health. We shall easily get a pass to travel, for it is also under French control (at least for the present, though after your news I have hopes that that situation may soon change) and probably we will even have a French guard to accompany us. I have not cultivated Monsieur Thierry for nothing."

He was frowning heavily, for there was much truth in what she was saying, little though he wanted to admit it. For her part, she seemed to regard his wrestle with himself with some amusement, for she was watching him with that engaging twinkle in her eyes again.

Nevertheless, the thing was ridiculous. "I think you little consider the danger you would be risking," he said shortly. "Besides, you could not hope to travel fast enough in a heavy coach. No, no, I thank you for the offer, but it will not do."

"What you mean is you want all the excitement for yourself!" she countered. "It shall take us no more than two days on the road, for I am known to dislike tedious journeys; and once in Salamanca, I shall contrive to deliver your message soon enough. I shall beg a passe-partout from Monsieur Thierry, and shall ride out of town to inspect the countryside and shake off the kinks of the journey. My dear sir, there shall not be the least danger. I am well known to be friendly with the French, and they are far too gallant to ever suspect a woman. I shall be far safer than you would be, in fact. I made up my mind yesterday it was the only answer, and indeed my only worry has been what to do with you while we are gone. But I think I have solved even that problem satisfactorily. Father Gregorio has already consented to hide you until you are recovered fully, and he may be trusted, believe me."

He wondered if it was the concussion that made him consider her preposterous proposal even for a moment. Every instinct was against it, for what she made sound so simple he knew to be an enterprise of considerable danger and inconvenience.

As if sensing he was weakening, she said persuasively, "And I have another reason as well why I may prove even more useful than you would have, in this particular case. I take it Wellington plans an advance in the north, and you were sent to discover the disposition of the town? If so, who could know that better than someone who has lived here for some years?"

Before he could answer, she added irrepressibly, "And I have further information that may well be of use to the

British army. Rumor has it the French marshals are expecting some such advance, but are arguing among themselves about the direction it will take. But—and this is the important part—Joseph Bonaparte—I refuse to call him King Joseph!—is said to be vastly annoyed that his brother has removed 27,000 of his experienced veterans for the Russian campaign just when Wellington looks to be moving into Spain at last. I had that from Monsieur Thierry himself, by the way, so it must be true."

He frowned. "Yes, we had heard that as well, but it is good to have it confirmed."

"I told you my friendship with him has proven useful on occasion."

She looked so smug he had to smile, but he shook his head as well. "It merely increases the urgency for my message to get through. But grateful as I am to you, I cannot let you take such a risk. That damn accident!" he fretted. "I never thought to be laid low like the veriest Johnny Raw by so ignoble a mishap, when so much depended on me! It should be a lesson to me not to think myself invincible."

"And yet it seems you are still making that mistake," she retorted.

He was too weak and in too much pain to guard his tongue. "It is my duty, and I have never yet shirked that, ma'am!" he snapped. "I have already informed you that my information is vital. The success of the entire campaign may rest upon it. Nor is this a time for amateur heroics."

"Ouch!" she said ruefully. "But it seems to me you believe yourself the only patriot, my dear Major. You are allowed to risk danger for something you believe in, but I am not. Is that it?"

He took advantage of her generous permission to swear, wishing he were not so damnably weak. "Hell and the devil confound it! It's bad enough I should have been undone by so stupid and careless a mishap, but I won't be responsible for the ruin of anyone else. And at least I knew what I was letting myself in for when I became a soldier."

"And as a soldier, you must be the first to see that the importance of vital information getting through outweighs any personal vanity," she informed him.

He closed his eyes, knowing himself too weary to argue any further. It seemed to him she had somehow rolled him up, horse, foot, and guns, when he had never dreamed of giving his consent to so dangerous a scheme. He knew he should protest further, but it was beyond his limited strength at the moment, and besides, he strongly suspected she would merely counter those arguments as easily as she had countered the ones he had already made. She was indeed quite a girl, Miss Regina Alderstock.

As if sensing she had won, she rose and said briskly, "And now I have teased you enough for one day. And I must not keep Monsieur de Thierry waiting. I shall be needing his signature on my travel documents. Now get some sleep, and stop looking as if the weight of the world were on your shoulders."

She would have left him then, but he opened his eyes and unexpectedly possessed himself of her hand. She did not resist, but stood regarding him with a slightly quizzical look in her eyes.

Abruptly he raised her hand to his lips and kissed it. "I should not be agreeing to this," he said unwillingly. "And you are more than remarkable, my girl. The Spanish don't know what they're overlooking."

She laughed and lightly released her hand. "No such thing. I just have a liking for getting my own way," she admitted in amusement. "Now, get some sleep. We have much to do in the morning."

She was gone on the words, before he could thank her any more, or think of anything further to say in protest of what he knew to be a dangerously mad scheme.

He had no intention, of course, of really giving his consent. He went to sleep on the determination not to allow her to shoulder his burdens, however remarkable she might be.

Accurate information was the backbone of Wellington's successes in the Peninsula, for his victories frequently rested on his ability to know when to offer battle and when to prudently retreat, and that required knowledge of the enemy's movements and strengths, and even their state of mind where possible. He would be on the fret already for news of the state of preparedness in Burgos, his ultimate objective, and whence any relief of Salamanca would come. He would expect his most reliable intelligence officer to get it through to him quickly, despite any unexpected mishaps, and certainly not to trust it to a slip of a girl, however brave and determined she might be.

But at that point in his cogitations the heavy sleep he seemed prone to since his accident firmly overtook him. And though the conviction remained with him when he woke the next morning, somehow, without his quite knowing how, he found himself thoroughly outgunned from the start. He had meant to firmly put an end to any such wild and dangerous scheme, but he somehow found it quite impossible to halt the juggernaut once it had started, which was a new experience for him.

Reggie herself brought his breakfast to him at an early hour, saying immediately, "I must not linger, for we are in a bustle of preparations and my absence will be marked. Monsieur de Thierry obligingly provided the passports, and even a guard, as I suspected he would. He even expressed a mild desire to accompany me, which is why I am in so great a hurry to be off, for he is tied up for the next day or two and is obliged to remain here, thank goodness. I need not tell you he would be very much in the way. Conchita is more than willing to come with me, and Father Gregorio will be here after dark tonight to fetch you. Do you think you will be able to walk by then? He dare not bring anyone to help carry you, I'm afraid."

"Of course I can walk!" he told her impatiently. "But my dear girl—"

But she was not listening to him. "I think I have made all

the necessary arrangements. You see there is *some* advantage to being dictatorial. With any luck we shall make Valladolid by nightfall. Poor Conchita! She is the one who is making a sacrifice, for she hates being rattled to death in fast carriages, and is likely to be black-and-blue by the time we arrive. In fact I would leave her behind, poor girl, except that she is my excuse for going at all. So you see, all that remains is for you to give me the message you want passed on, and I shall guarantee to deliver it."

He saw that she was indeed determined, and though it went much against the grain with him, he acknowledged that she was right. He would be of little use in his present state, and the importance of his information was such that all other considerations must be put aside for the moment. Besides, he had by then developed enough faith in her determination and courage that he did not really much doubt that she would do exactly what she said she would. He would back her against the French any day.

He had some slight doubts remaining that she would be able to master the gist of his message without having to write it down, which would be far too dangerous. But he soon saw that he had again underestimated her. She showed a lively grasp of the fortifications of the town, and would in some way be able to give more information than he would have been able to collect in a day. She also betrayed an unfeminine knowledge of such technical matters as munitions and artillery, and betrayed an excellent memory for figures.

It was only as she was preparing to take her leave of him, betraying no other emotion than a certain haste, that he fully realized for the first time that he might never see her again. He would be long gone before she could return, and though at the moment Wellington was planning to move on the north, that could change in an instant. Besides, he had spent too many years in the army not to know that the fortunes of war were such they both might be dead tomorrow.

He halted her in the middle of some last-minute instructions to say abruptly, "Yes, I shall do as Father Gregorio says and not take any unnecessary risks. You need not worry about me, you absurd girl. And I should know by now that you take all this as the merest commonplace, and have no desire to be treated as a heroine, or even thanked. But you must know how aware I am of the danger you are undertaking, and of the enormity of my debt to you. On all counts!"

"Well, if you are minded to be a dead bore, I shall take my leave of you," she countered, on the verge of doing so.

He smiled ruefully. "Yes, you must. If you are to do this thing there is no time for delay. But I—" He shook his head, and abruptly captured her hand and again raised it to his lips. "I can only repeat, you are quite a girl. I shall hope to see you again in more ordinary circumstances."

Then he frowned. "Which reminds me, it would not do for you and your sister to linger too long in Salamanca. With any luck—and the information you carry getting successfully through—we may be in position to attack by the end of the month. In fact, I would be a great deal easier in my mind to know you were safely back in England. You may have been out of the war till now, aside from the French occupation, but if we are successful that shall no longer be the case. We mean to take Spain, whatever it costs, and drive the French back into their own country. Wellington will never rest until he has accomplished that, whatever they may think at home."

"I pray God he may succeed," she said soberly. "But as for my safety, nonsense! Anyway, my stepfather is too ill to make such a journey, so there is an end to the discussion. We shall do very well, I promise you, for we are safe enough under French hands, and if you do succeed in driving them out, we shall be even better. So you see there is no need to worry."

He was far from satisfied and thought her too naive, for all her determination and courage, to understand the realities of war. Memories of the atrocities that took place after the successful reductions of Badajoz and Ciudad Rodrigo, where no woman was safe and the men wholly beyond the control of their officers, made his blood run cold. He would have to have a talk with Father Gregorio and see if he could make her see reason.

It was her turn to hesitate for a moment, and for the first time since he had known her she looked a little uncertain. "Well, I must be off. Oh dear, I hate goodbyes! Especially since you have reminded me we might never see each other again after today. You will—you will take care of yourself, won't you? Remember, I have a considerable investment in you by this time, and I would hate to see all my handiwork go to waste."

He smiled and discovered he had retained his grip on her hand. "We shall meet again, never fear," he said confidently. "I must confess you have confounded all my former prejudices. I have never thought war a business for women, but you prove to me that a woman can be every bit as brave as a man, and as patriotic. I shall never forget you, Reggie Alderstock."

Almost unconsciously he increased his pressure on her hand and pulled her down to him. She blushed a little, but did not resist, and offered her lips willingly for his kiss.

He had intended the most innocent of embraces, but was surprised at the sudden uprush of emotion he experienced as his lips touched hers. He had admired her and found her both amusing and frequently exasperating, not to mention possessed of an astonishing amount of resource and courage. But he had not thought of her in a romantic vein. He had been too ill and too worried to consider such possibilities, and it would have been the work of a blackguard to betray her trust and help by taking advantage of her.

But now his hand tightened as of its own accord, and he had to steel himself not to betray the sudden hunger he felt. For all her composure he suspected she was still an innocent, and he would be a fool indeed to create a situation they could neither of them afford.

Besides, he cynically mistrusted the drama of the moment. He had an equally strong prejudice against the likelihood of wartime romances surviving past the touching moment of parting. He might have experienced an uprush of emotion in that kiss that surprised him, but it would be madness to read anything more into it than gratitude and admiration for her courage. They had been thrown together in the most unlikely and intimate of circumstances, and reacted as any two healthy and reasonably attractive people would have.

And if nothing else, he could not afford to invest any more in it. That sounded callous, but it was the truth. Despite what she thought, she was likely to be in considerable danger soon enough, and he could not do his job if he had her safety forever preying on his mind. He had seen too many good officers spoiled by having their loyalty divided, having to worry about their wives as well as their men. He had no intention of allowing it to happen to him.

All the same, when she had released herself and gone quickly from the room without another word, he found himself regretting that there could be no more to it. She had aroused his admiration and liking in a way few women had ever been able to do, and it would be a shame indeed if they should never meet again.

Chapter 7

August, 1812
Madrid

TWO MONTHS LATER, on August 12, the British army rode in triumph into Madrid.

Reggie was there to see it, as she had not been to see their equally triumphant entry into Salamanca, due perhaps in some small part to the information she herself had carried.

Her farewell to Major Adam Canfield had been harder than she had anticipated. She had halted just outside his door, a frown between her brows, and a hand raised rather tremulously to her mouth, which still carried the warmth of his kiss.

Only when she realized what she was doing did she shake herself sharply and hurry on about her business. Even less than the major could she afford to invest any sentimentality into their parting. She did not deceive herself that the chances of their ever meeting again were strong. And, isolated as she was from her own countrymen, she had far more to lose than he did by reading more into the situation than was warranted by the somewhat unusual and romantic circumstances.

In short it would be folly indeed to allow herself to fall in love with Major Adam Canfield, however attractive and personable he might be. And she was too honest to deny to herself that she was in very real danger of doing just that.

The journey to deliver his message had been as uneventful as she had anticipated. The French were generally gallant, and the French commandant had provided them with an escort, exactly as she had foreseen. It was but one of the more ironic aspects of their journey.

During that first day on the road it had been hard to believe that two vast opposing armies could be anywhere in the vicinity, for there was no sign of anything but the usual peaceful countryside. They had broken their journey at Valladolid on that first night, which Maria, being Burgos-born, pronounced a filthy and flea-ridden village of neither beauty nor interest. But they were all by then so exhausted by the many hours of being jolted over inferior roads that not even Maria objected to the inn they had put up in, or did more than inspect the sheets with a sniff.

Only Reggie, her mind still overstimulated and her body exhausted, found it difficult to sleep. Surrounded on one side by the snores of the nurse, and on the other by Conchita's softer breathing, she lay awake for a long time, unable to keep the happenings of the last few days from replaying themselves in her mind. Or to wonder if the major were lying awake at that moment, too, thinking of her.

Then, annoyed with herself for the absurd trend of her thoughts, she firmly turned over and settled herself for sleep.

They reached Salamanca in the late afternoon of the next day, and armed with Monsieur de Thierry's passport were admitted into the town without difficulty. And at least there the signs of war were more obvious. If Reggie had thought Burgos full of French soldiers, their number paled before those in Salamanca. Everywhere one looked were blue uniforms, and the ground outside the walls of the town was crowded with tents and campfires and loafing *carabinieres*, some looking little more than children.

They had not been in the city for much more than an hour before she learned the reason for this unexpected concentration. Marshal Marmont, retreating before the British advance with his entire French Army of Portugal, had been forced to fall back on Salamanca. And still more important for her purposes, it was rumored that the English army was even then within five miles of the city.

Her heart had swelled at the news, but there were preliminaries to be got through first before she could hope to deliver her message. Conchita's aunt had been discovered to be on the mend, and indeed much surprised and touched by this unexpected display of familial devotion. She welcomed them effusively and seemed not overly disturbed by the imminent threat of an English invasion. She shrugged her plump shoulders philosophically and pronounced that English, French, it made little difference, except that they said the English paid for what they took, which would be a pleasant change, and no one would be sorry to see the despised French depart.

Maria had graciously consented to be pleased with Salamanca, which boasted wide boulevards and beautiful houses as well as excellent shops. For her part Reggie was far more interested in the country outside the city's walls. The city was surrounded by low hills, and it was unexpectedly stirring for her to think the English army under Wellington might be just over one of those rises. It somehow made the liberation of Spain more real to her, as if it might actually be possible, not just some long-prayed-for dream.

She had ridden out the next morning, to her hostess's scarcely concealed astonishment, on a borrowed horse and alone. To Conchita's patient explanation that the English were very much addicted to such exercise and their women used to far more freedom than were allowed young Spanish girls, Dona Luisa shook her head, as if to say that all foreigners were crazy. But she resignedly saw to the loan of a horse and asked no questions, content to sit exchanging the latest gossip with her niece, and wholly ignoring the stirring events going on just outside her heavily curtained windows.

The gentle Conchita had been by no means as content to see Reggie go off alone, and would have insisted upon accompanying her had not Reggie pointed out, truthfully, that her stepsister was no horsewoman, and that she was far better occupied keeping her aunt's curiosity at bay.

And in truth Reggie had received nothing more than a few curious stares. Once through the gates of the town, she had ridden in a roundabout way toward the hills where she trusted the British army was encamped. She was not aware of any particular fear, for there was little enough risk in her undertaking. In fact, her predominant emotion had been a certain unquenchable excitement. It seemed she had spent far too many years sitting out the war, and was more than happy to have a more active part at last.

For safety's sake she had prepared a story in case she was challenged or accosted by the French, but she had not needed it. In fact the only risk she had run was of drowning, for upon approaching the British lines, she discovered a considerable river lay in her path that had to be forded.

Her borrowed mount with its cumbersome Spanish lady's saddle did not take kindly to the idea, and she had at first feared she had come all that way only to fail ignominiously at the end for want of a resolute enough horse. That thought made her angry, and she used her whip and heels ruthlessly, determined to swim across if necessary. But fortunately in the end she was able to force her reluctant mount into the water.

The river proved to be running faster than she had expected, and her nervous mount was soon up to his shoulders, thoroughly wetting her skirts. That didn't matter, of course, especially on such a hot day, but she knew her first real fear then, for her stupid horse seemed in danger of losing its head completely and heading off downstream, which would probably mean the end of both of them. But by dint of much urging and clinging to the saddle, while her horse half walked, half swam across the raging torrent, showing the whites of his eyes in fear the whole way, she managed to get them both across at last.

It was then the two British soldiers found her. The sight of their familiar red uniforms had filled her with unexpected emotion, but that was nothing to what they seemed to be experiencing at the sight of a lone female approaching their lines. They were at first amazed that she had crossed so swollen a river on her own, and then, when she spoke in English to them, their astonishment seemed to be complete. But they had recovered quickly enough, and willingly escorted her back to their lines, where the major had given her a name to ask for.

It had sent a further thrill up her spine when she had first seen the British army spread out below before her. It seemed to go on forever, and she had looked about her in growing fascination as they rode through the camp. It was like a huge movable city, for everywhere were dusty tents, and spring wagons piled with supplies or munitions, and horses and mules contentedly cropping what little grass there was in the baked June earth.

The men absorbed her attention even more. For the first time in far too many years she was surrounded by her own countrymen: a sea of rough soldiers with sunburnt faces, all in shabby scarlet jackets whose silver buttons were tarnished black and whose shakos retained very little shape after long years in that hostile climate. Now and then she caught sight of a green uniform belonging to a rifleman, or the half forgotten insignia of the Guards. They were all busy about their own affairs, lounging and smoking before their fires, or off on some duty or other.

She was unprepared for the sting of tears the sight had roused in her and had had to hastily blink them away. The uprush of homesickness she felt then had surprised her, for it had been a long time since she had thought of herself as English.

But after that the actual delivery of her message had

tended to be merely anticlimactic. She had soon found herself confronting a tall and ugly captain who regarded her with the blankest astonishment; then when he heard what she had to say, he jumped up as though electrified.

He had asked her a few short, sharp questions about Adam, then in turn hurried away to pass on her information, giving her an inkling of how important it was. He had left her in the care of two attractive young officers who professed to be friends of the major's and to her amusement insisted upon giving her tea.

Over that most English of meals they plied her with questions and amusing chatter, reminding her poignantly of her father's young assistants so many years ago. In their presence the years had unaccountably fallen away from her, stirring memories she had thought long forgotten in the aftermath of tragedy and war.

The only difficult part of the whole had been everyone's embarrassing insistence upon treating her as something of a heroine, which she knew she was not. And she had had to say goodbye to her new acquaintances far too soon, for she dared not be out after the gates of the city closed for the night.

Captain Prescott had escorted her back as far as the river, unconsciously repeating the major's warning that a battle was imminent and that she and her stepsister would do better to remove to Burgos—or even leave the country altogether.

She thanked him and did not bother to explain why she could not take such excellent advice. Her last sight of the cheerful camp had been of the sea of shabby red uniforms and her new friends waving cheerfully to her: young men of good family, like Major Canfield, who had endured years of danger for their country, and who, far from complaining, laughed and made light of the many inconveniences and shifts they were put to. She had somehow not anticipated how difficult it would be for her to turn her back on it all and ride back alone toward the French and her own suddenly far less welcome responsibilities.

But normality had soon enough reasserted itself, as she had known it would. They had remained in Salamanca only a week longer, for Conchita was anxious about her father. If Conchita's aunt had been bewildered by this whirlwind visit, she did not betray it in her tearful goodbyes, and the return journey had been as uneventful as the way out.

Nor was Reggie particularly surprised, when they at last reached Burgos again, to discover that her patient had left some days ago.

Father Gregorio had shaken his head over it, for he had not believed him well enough to travel. But the major had been adamant and had set out on the priest's old mule less than a week after they themselves had departed. His concussion seemed gone, and his ribs were mending, and if he could not use his left arm and had had to have it supported in a sling to be able to endure the jolts of the road, the old priest had been unable to convince him to remain even a few more days.

As to his ultimate fate, Father Gregorio knew nothing more than that his mule had been found the next morning, grazing peacefully outside the gates of the city, and been returned to him, so that they must trust to God's mercy that all was well.

And that had seemed to close the book on so exciting a chapter in her life. Reggie had thanked the kindly priest, and with a faint sigh returned to her everyday life. No good would be served by dwelling on what might have been, or wishing that they might have met under less dramatic circumstances.

And by dint of much sensible advice to herself, gradually even the memory of his kiss no longer had the power to halt her in her tracks, only to find herself some moments later with not the slightest idea what it was she had been doing.

And ordinary life was demanding enough at the moment. It was not until some days after their return that she discov-

ered Marshal Marmont had abandoned the city of Salamanca without a shot being fired, only a few days after she
and Conchita had left it, and that the British had ridden in
in triumph amid the shouts and vivas of the inhabitants.
That had caused a certain momentary bitterness; nor could
she help wondering if Major Adam Canfield was safely
back with his regiment and even then being feted by all the
prettiest girls in Salamanca.

But she was sensible enough not to indulge in such useless repinings. At any rate, while she remained tied to Burgos, and it remained under French rule, she could not afford
to be seen to be on good terms with the British, or remind
the powers-that-be that she was herself English and thus
technically an enemy.

And events had soon gone more or less back to normal
after that. For a while there was some fear that the British
meant to continue their advance and attack Burgos itself;
and she did not know whether to be glad or sorry that in the
end the threat did not materialize.

For some weeks all they received were rumors of much
maneuvering between the two armies, in and around Salamanca, while neither side seemed eager to engage in a
pitched battle.

In the meantime, Conchita was formally betrothed to a
young man belonging to a wealthy and prominent Spanish
family. The engagement had been in negotiation for some
months, in the accepted Spanish fashion, and she herself
seemed shyly happy. She was to travel to Madrid for her
betrothal festivities, and would not hear of going without
her dearest Reggie to accompany her.

Thus it was that Reggie had found herself on the road to
Madrid when the bloody and terrible battle of Salamanca at
last took place.

The news that reached them on the road was only
sketchy at best, and caused her a number of sleepless
nights. They had reached Madrid before they learned that
Wellington had achieved a stunning victory over the vastly

superior French forces outside of Salamanca, on the very heights Reggie had herself seen so long ago.

It was stirring enough news; but it was long before she was able to learn any more than the bare outlines of the engagement. What regiments were involved on the British side, or what casualties there had been—they were rumored to be high on both sides—no one seemed to know; and it was impossible not to remember her new friends, those charming young soldiers, or consider with a pang that some of them might even then be dead.

As for Major Canfield, she could only pray that his injuries had kept him out of the battle, a devout hope that she knew instinctively he would not share.

And in those long anxious days an unwelcome truth was thrust upon her. It seemed that never again would the war be just a distant horror to her. It was all very well to talk of being sensible. Probably she would never see any of them again. And yet their deaths would grieve her nonetheless.

Chapter 8

To HER INTENSE surprise and delight, Reggie saw Major Canfield just two days later.

Madrid, which she knew well, had been as hot and airless as usual. Conchita's new relations proved kind, if decidedly straitlaced, and her fiancé was a charming young man who openly adored her. They all found Reggie somewhat unexpected, but did their best to make her feel welcome.

But Reggie, hedged round by the strict Spanish customs and for Conchita's sake denied her usual outlets, found herself thinking more and more longingly of her adventure. It was as if the taste of it had made her resent even more the role usually allotted to women. Stirring events were even then taking place, and she must remain on the sidelines, chatting of polite nothings to formal strangers in hot airless rooms. It sometimes seemed to her that men were but greedy creatures, keeping all the adventures to themselves.

But they had their own considerable excitement to liven the tedium of Madrid. For after the British victory at Salamanca, King Joseph, fearing to remain so exposed, had withdrawn from the capital, and Wellington had immediately marched south to occupy it instead of pursuing his victories in the north.

The long-tried Madrilenes had rushed out to welcome the British in an excess of hysterical joy. Ten miles outside the city the weary British troops were met by huge crowds, singing and dancing and bearing all sorts of delicacies and wine. Women strewed the road with palm leaves and ran among the highly embarrassed troops, kissing their hands and weeping with gratitude. All the church bells rang continuously, and it seemed as if the entire population were in the streets to welcome the conquering heroes.

Reggie, condemned to watch it all from a discreet balcony among Conchita's highly proper relations, longed to be down in the streets dancing with the rest. To see the British army come marching in filled her with a swelling pride, nor could she help wondering if her major were down among that mass of humanity. Was some more lucky female kissing him even now, as she had watched countless women do, pulling him down from his saddle to reach him, and laughing as she tossed her flowers up to him?

It was a picture that caused her a considerable pang. Nor could she quite quell her envy as she watched the citizens cast rose petals for the British officers' horses to tread on, nor could she keep herself from scanning the laughing ranks of sunburnt troops for one distinctive figure she had seen only sick and gray with pain, but that she thought she would recognize anywhere.

After that joyous welcome, a ball was given in Wellington's honor to celebrate his tremendous victories, to which all of wealthy Madrid had been invited. Reggie, bidden to attend with her distinguished hosts, was aware of a distinct acceleration of her usually steady pulse at the prospect, and took more than usual care about her appearance, scoffing at herself even as she did so.

Privately she thought Conchita, dressed in the height of Spanish fashion with a high comb in her hair, completely outshone her; but she had a French gown she had never yet worn, of some soft cobwebby stuff in an ethereal white that became her far better than she knew, and effectively stood out amidst the blacks of the matrons and the red of the British uniforms.

And it was impossible to deny to herself any longer the excitement she felt as she stood in the crowded ballroom, already raised to the sweltering point by the number of people packed into it and the hundreds of candles in chandeliers and sconces all around the room, all adding to the natural heat of a hot August night.

But few appeared to notice the heat or allow it to impair their enjoyment of the glittering evening. A good many of the perspiring guests were in full British dress uniform, their brightly polished silver buttons and sword hilts gleaming in the candlelight, the martial colors clashing with the stiff silks and laces of the Spanish ladies in their mantillas and high combs. A polyglot babble added to the confusion, for she heard Spanish, French, and English spoken all around her, punctuating the beat of the music to which whirling couples danced and glided.

All in all it was an impressive scene, and standing beside her stiff hosts, Reggie anxiously scanned the crowd for a familiar face. Conchita, beside her, was tapping her foot under her stiff petticoats to the music and trying not to look as if she would give anything to be off dancing with her dashing fiancé. Her stern mama-in-law-to-be had not yet released them to the dancing and was introducing the blushing Conchita to a series of important personages, all from old and extremely noble Spanish families.

It was then, as Reggie stood with only half an ear tuned to the heavy compliments, that a tall figure on the other side of the room caught her eye. He stood a head above most of the people in that room, and made her heart suddenly skip a beat, for he looked hauntingly familiar, despite having his back turned toward her, and despite the many weeks that had passed since she had last seen him.

But even as her excitement rose she told herself sternly not to be a fool. Ten to one Major Adam Canfield was a hundred miles away at that very moment—if indeed he was still alive. At any rate, it was ridiculous to suppose she would be able to pick him out so instinctively in such a crowd. She scarcely knew him, after all.

But even as she was deriding herself, the figure turned,

and she caught sight of a profile there could be no mistaking. He was in conversation with a comely señorita in the elaborate comb and mantilla of the wealthy Spaniards, bending his tall head slightly as her flashing eyes flirted up at him.

As Reggie caught her breath, stirred by a jealousy as immediate as it was ludicrous, he looked up, as if feeling her glancing at him from across the room. His eyes widened, as if he, too, were seeing a ghost, and he seemed to have halted in midsentence, for the girl at his side laughed up at him and playfully tapped him with her fan. At that he seemed to catch himself up and finished what he had been saying, though his eyes remained incredulously on Reggie through the shifting throng of dancers.

A moment later he smoothly made his apologies to his disappointed companion and was coming quickly across the room, his progress easily traceable among the other revelers by his great height. Reggie found herself unexpectedly breathless and was surprised now that she had recognized him at all, for he was a very different creature from the gray-faced but determinedly cheerful man she had last seen. In place of the dirty and bloodstained garb of the Spanish peasant, he wore his dashing Hussar uniform with the fur-trimmed pelisse thrown carelessly over one shoulder. It reminded her that she had always thought it unfair for a uniform to be so very attractive. His white breeches were spotless, and his Hessians unbelievably highly polished, while his face seemed more deeply tanned than ever and alive with vitality, so that his blue eyes were almost startling in contrast. Even his dark curls had been ruthlessly tamed, so that there was no trace of her ragged patient left to be seen in his splendid figure.

One or two persons tried to speak to him, but he was evidently not to be deterred, for he briefly shook his head and passed on.

She tried sensibly and belatedly to order her errant pulse to behave itself. It had naturally occurred to her that he might be there, and she did not trouble to deny to herself that she had worn the expensive white gown with that possibility in mind. But it was absurd to make anything more of it than a casual meeting between old acquaintances who had been thrown briefly together. Anything other than that was too dangerous.

But the light in his eyes did not support that sensible theory. She watched him approach her, feeling suddenly absurdly shy, for there was no mistaking the pleasure or astonishment in his face.

"Good God, it *is* you!" he exclaimed, reaching her and catching both of her hands in his, wholly impervious to the patent disapproval of the rigid matron beside her. "I could scarcely believe my eyes when I looked up and saw you."

She feared she was blushing betrayingly, but said quickly in warning, "Yes, indeed it is. How wonderful to see you again after all these years, Major. But you have not met my sister, I believe, and I must make you known to Dona Francisca, who is soon to be her mother-in-law."

But she saw she need not have worried, for his wits were as sharp as ever, and his manners excellent. He bowed elegantly over Dona Francisca's hand, addressing her in fluent Spanish that had her unbending a little from her first sharp-eyed suspicion; then he turned to Conchita as to a stranger, instead of someone he had last seen bending over his sickbed adjusting his pillows, and warmly congratulated her on her engagement.

Conchita was having trouble hiding a laugh, and there was a decided twinkle in the back of his eyes as well; but he somehow contrived to make it appear to Dona Francisca that he was an old and valued friend of Reggie's family. In fact he soon had that starched-up dame almost eating out of his hand, so that she forgot whatever suspicions she might have had about how her unusual English guest might have managed to renew her acquaintance with a British soldier, living as she did in a French-occupied town.

He soon requested and received gracious permission to

lead Reggie into the next dance, and said in English, as he at last led her away, "Whew! That was a close one. Some intelligence officer I am, but I confess I was so startled to see you that for the moment everything else flew completely out of my head."

"Yes, but you recovered yourself very well," she told him in amusement. "In fact, I was impressed by your coolness under fire, Major. Dona Francisca terrifies me. But are you sure you should be dancing?"

"Why on earth should I not—oh, you mean my wounds! Good Lord, I have long forgotten those." He proved it by showing himself an excellent dancer. "But, my dearest Reggie—"

Then he broke off, grinning, and apologized. "Your unexpected appearance seems to have knocked all my manners straight out of my head. And I seem to remember I displayed few enough of them the last time we met. *Miss Alderstock*, I should doubtless have said."

"No, why?" she countered, feeling absurdly happy. "Everyone calls me Reggie. And you must admit our acquaintance, to date, has not been marked by its conventionality."

He grinned. "That, at least, is true. In fact, I blush to think what light I must have appeared to you in. And I must confess I have been thinking of you as Reggie all these months. But first, tell me what you are doing in Madrid. I could scarcely believe my eyes when I looked up and caught sight of you across the room."

"Oh, we are becoming quite cosmopolitan these days. We are here to attend Conchita's engagement festivities. But I must admit we little expected to find the British army marching in within days of our arrival."

"No, or we to be here. Life is never dull in the army at least. But I am more than delighted to see you here. I have had some sleepless nights since last we parted. I can only think it was the concussion that made me agree to so outrageous a scheme. I knew of course that you reached the camp safely, for I heard all about your visit. But I have been on pins and needles to know you were safely home again. You had no trouble?"

"None at all, I promise you. And it would seem my heroic gesture was but little needed, after all. You must have reached the army not many days after I did."

"Never think it," he said, smiling warmly down at her. "You are indeed a heroine, as most of my friends will attest. And I fear I never even thanked you properly for all you did for me."

"Oh, pooh. That is past history, and thus no longer of interest. I am merely delighted to discover you are still in one piece. Having patched you back together once, I discover I have developed a proprietorial interest in seeing you remain that way. But you came through the late battle unscathed, I see?"

"Not even a scratch. At any rate, you should know by now I bear a charmed life."

"Yes, I could see the results of it the last time we met," she retorted.

He laughed ruefully. "Don't remind me. I have yet to live that down, believe me. Of all the ignominious mishaps! But at the risk of earning your displeasure by appearing boring, I must at least thank you once for all you risked for me. And speaking of which, I was serious. You have become something of a legend in the army, did you know? I returned not only to find my information already received and acted on, but everyone talking of the remarkable Miss Alderstock. Prescott could not sing your praises highly enough, and he was by no means the only one. Two others of my friends swear they lost their hearts to you, and more importantly, that they gave you tea and company during your visit to the camp, for which I was grateful to them. I was also deucedly jealous, I confess, for I had come to think of you as uniquely my own property. But I could not deny that you were indeed a complete heroine."

So much for all her sensible lectures. She did not even

object to this remarkably exaggerated statement, or the oddly possessive tone in his voice. "Pray don't put such nonsense into the mouth of your excellent colonel, for he never said anything of the sort, I'll be bound," was all she said. "Heroine indeed! I was never in the slightest danger, and did only what anyone else would have done under the circumstances. More than that, I enjoyed myself hugely. But I am delighted to see you are fully recovered from your accident and looking so well. There was no lasting damage?"

"Good God, no! Barring a slightly stiff shoulder now and then," he assured her. "And I won't try any longer to thank you, since it so obviously embarrasses you, except to say that my services are yours to command at any time you should be in need of them. But at least you must permit me to say how beautiful you are looking tonight, and how delighted I am to see you."

She blushed and laughed. She knew she looked well, for her white gown with its shimmering overdress, fastened at the front and down the bodice with pearls, was straight from Paris and had never been worn. More, she had piled up her dark curls with pearls scattered throughout and had allowed one glossy ringlet to fall forward onto her bare shoulder, a new and daring style that had made Conchita profess herself wild with envy, for in the presence of her strict mother-in-law, it was one she dared not copy.

But Reggie at least made an effort to hang on to the dregs of common sense. "Yes, there is something to be said for maintaining good relations with the French. But I fear we poor women are all undone by this sea of gorgeous scarlet. Not that it isn't wonderful to see after the surfeit of French blue I have been surrounded by for so long."

He sobered immediately. "Yes, I am longing to hear about everything that has been happening. I promise you have been much on my mind. Did you—?"

But he was not allowed to finish his sentence. There was an exclamation behind them, and a vaguely familiar voice cried, "By all that's holy, it's our little heroine! Adam, you dog, how dare you serve us such a trick! Why didn't you tell us Miss Alderstock would be here? In fact, I call it devilish unkind of you to try to tip us a rise like that!"

The speaker was the good-looking young lieutenant who had amused her with his tales of camp life on that day so long ago. He was accompanied by another, older officer with a lively, attractive face, who said pityingly, "He served us such a trick, my poor innocent, because he had no intention of sharing his prize with us."

"At least you have that right," retorted Adam. "Go away, both of you. Can't you see you're not wanted here?"

"Miss Alderstock!" appealed the insouciant young lieutenant, resplendent in full-dress uniform and a pair of heroic ginger whiskers and looking to be no more than eighteen or nineteen years old. "I appeal to your sense of fair play. Who was it that entertained you while this lazy fellow was lounging in bed, leaving you to do his dangerous work for him? In fact, he is clearly not worthy of your notice."

"A little more of that, infant, and I shall be tempted to tip you out the nearest window," warned Adam, adding for her benefit, "I must apologize for my friends, Miss Alderstock. It would seem army life has robbed them of what few manners they once possessed."

"Ah, I have clearly touched a nerve!" grinned the lieutenant. "As for tipping me out a window, it would puzzle you to find one open. I tried to prize one open a few minutes ago, for the room feels like nothing so much as a steambath, and I've been regretting this dashed high collar of mine for the past hour and more. But you'd have thought I had proposed an indecent act, the scandalized stares I received. It beats me how they do it, for most of 'em are even more cursedly overdressed than we are. But that's neither here nor there. You must know, Miss Alderstock, that Adam here fancies himself invincible. It was good to see him felled by so humble and humbling a mishap, and we don't intend to allow him soon to forget it."

"Now that I cannot allow," she interposed in amusement, enjoying their nonsense. "I suspect the major did not tell you that he suffered that mishap in rescuing a child from being crushed to death. I don't consider that in the least humbling."

"You are wasting your breath, my dear," said the major resignedly. "I warned you I shall never succeed in living it down. And I see that I have no need to present to you Captain Robert Colville and Lieutenant Lord George Austerby, two of my so-called friends, though I am beginning to wonder about that, at least."

"Very much at your service, Miss Alderstock," put in the older man, shaking her hand. "Only Adam would have the good fortune not only to be rescued by the only Englishwoman in five hundred miles, but an exceedingly charming one as well."

"Yes, and what's more, Adam here meant to keep her all to himself," said young Lord George gaily. "I don't know what he deserves for that. Yes, I do! She shall dance with each of us, in turn. That will teach him to play such a shabby trick on us."

"It will indeed. But in that case you may settle it among yourselves which of you is to be first while Miss Alderstock and I finish our dance," put in the major coolly, and ignoring their protests, led her firmly back onto the floor.

There he said feelingly, "Hell and the devil confound it. Now I have little hope of getting you to myself for as much as ten minutes. But I warned you that you had become something of a heroine with my friends, curse them for pushing in where they're not wanted."

No, Reggie acknowledged ruefully, she was decidedly long past any hope of common sense prevailing.

Chapter 9

ALL OF THEM did dance with her afterward, and a dozen more of Adam's friends besides.

It was heady stuff for a female who considered herself very much on the shelf—or it would have been had Reggie not known herself to be vastly in the minority as an Englishwoman at such a gathering. There were others present, the wives of officers who habitually followed the drum, and whom she might personally consider to lead far more interesting lives than her own. But it was very obvious that the young officers who surrounded her so eagerly found her own story the more romantic.

Nevertheless, she firmly closed her mind to such unpalatable truths, as well as to the fact that the inevitable return to her normal humdrum life was likely to be even harder to bear than it had been already, and she gave herself up to enjoyment. As for the almost certain disapproval of her hostess, and the likelihood that she was making herself the cynosure of all eyes, what were moonbeams and candlelight and music for, if one didn't become at least a little intoxicated? The memories were apt to have to last her for a very long time indeed.

The major, despite his protests, put up with the competition tolerantly enough. He endured much good-natured ribbing, and it was obvious he was a prime favorite. For her part, Reggie was introduced to so many attractive young officers that her head was soon spinning.

But if she had once reassured herself that her somewhat

breathless reaction to Major Adam Canfield was the inevitable result of the unusual circumstances in which they had met, and the length of time it had been since she had seen a personable young Englishman, she could no longer thus deceive herself. At the moment she was surrounded by personable young Englishmen, not a few far more conventionally attractive than the dark major. And it was an effort to disguise the sharp disappointment she experienced every time the arms surrounding her did not belong to Major Adam Canfield.

She was at least glad when conversation turned soon enough to the recent battle. Some remembered that Reggie had actually been on the heights of San Cristoval, where the battle ultimately took place, if only after much maneuvering by both armies.

"Maneuver! Don't even mention the word!" begged young Lord George. "If you can tell me what all that was in aid of, save a fine display on the art of moving armies senselessly about over some curst inhospitable country, I would be grateful to you. And just when I had begun to think we were settled in Salamanca for the duration, and had found a most charming companion to while away the hours with."

Someone else said in amusement, "And that was why we moved, once we'd reduced the forts. Old Hookey's no fool, and there was nothing to stay for, save all of us getting soft. Besides, his lordship thought to give the guerillas a chance to do some good for a change. Word is they intercepted so many enemy dispatches that we knew what the French were about to do before their officers did."

"If so, there's even less excuse for all that maneuvering," complained Lord George. "We could have remained where we were in comfort and waited for the French army to come back again, and I'd have been spared the worst case of sunburn I can remember in many a day."

Everyone laughed, for he had the sort of fair, freckled complexion that would inevitably burn. Adam said, "Wait until you've been a little longer out here, and have burnt to leather like the rest of us. But speaking of the guerillas, Miss Alderstock's stepbrother is with them, I understand."

Everyone regarded her with new interest. "They have our gratitude," said Captain Prescott in his kind way. "Nor do I envy them their task. Guerilla warfare is a curst lonely business."

"Filipe would be gratified to hear you say so," admitted Reggie. "But contrary to what I fear most of you think, the Spanish do boast their patriots, you know."

"Oh, Lord yes," agreed Captain Colville carelessly. "We've no quarrel with *them*. It's their generals who seem designed to make our lives difficult. Speaking of which, Marmont nearly put one over on us that time, I must admit. I feared for a bit that we were to be the ones romped, not the other way round."

Adam explained for Reggie's benefit, "After luring us all the way to the Douro, over some most inhospitable country, as Bantling says, he almost succeeded in turning our flank and did gain a day's march on us. It was touch and go for a while whether they'd beat us back to Salamanca, which would have made us all feel like fools."

"By Jove, yes. I won't forget those two days of forced marches in a hurry. The men began to claim we were running a race to see who could get back there first. We covered more than eighty miles in two days, Miss Alderstock—as the number of troops who fell out in exhaustion will attest. I admit I've spent more enjoyable times myself," confessed Captain Colville.

"Especially when we ended up back on the heights of San Cristoval, exactly where we'd started from. I began to believe both commanders had no intention of ever coming to grips with one another," complained Lord George.

"But then it began to rain like twenty kinds of hell, and I knew we'd be engaged by morning," said Captain Prescott.

Adam said, "You must know it rains before all of

Wellington's battles. Wellington weather, they call it. The men have come to expect it."

"They say Wellington is a master of defense, but after that let no man deny in my hearing that he can take the offensive when he wants to," said Captain Colville. "The French retreat looked more like a rout than anything I've seen in a long time."

"We lost five thousand men and five officers, while by most counts the French lost three times that, including Marshal Marmont himself wounded," explained Adam. "Near enough to a rout, as Colville says."

Reggie could not help but feel an uprush of pride, but it startled her to hear them speak so casually of what she guessed must have been a very bloody affair. It also startled her to realize how wonderful it felt to be among her own people again. She had not realized how much she had missed the English sense of humor, and their way of making light of the most serious matters. The English covered even tragedy with a jest as a way of coping, and it was something people used to weeping and wailing little understood.

"But you did not pursue your victory?" she asked curiously. "There was much rumor that you meant to push on straight to Burgos."

There was an exchange of pained looks. After a moment Adam spoke with a careful lack of emotion. "Through an unfortunate mixup with the Spanish troops left at Alba, the bulk of the French were allowed to escape. Anyway, we went as far as Valladolid, but thanks in part to the information you got through, Wellington chose not to invest Burgos itself at this time. We came here instead."

"Oh—dear," she said, understanding that the Spanish had, once more, failed in their commitments to the British army.

"Well, it can't be helped," said Adam philisophically. "Besides, it never does to second guess the outcome of anything in war. And that is enough talk of war and destruction. Now it is my dance again, I think, if you will all excuse us."

And to his friends' patent disappointment, he led her back onto the dance floor in time for a waltz.

Reggie gave herself up to the music, no longer even trying to pretend to herself she wasn't well away on the effects of moonbeams and foolish dreams. She had long since bid farewell to all common sense, and was aware only of a feeling of intense happiness. "Are all British officers such good dancers?" she remarked inconsequently.

"Oh, Lord yes. Most of us waste little time, whenever we are in a place for more than a few days, in giving a ball. We have had to learn to take our pleasure where we can find it. But I thought I'd never get you to myself again. In my opinion, I've been more than generous, but would you mind if we ducked out before they find us again? I really do want to talk to you."

She thought resignedly of her reputation with Conchita's in-laws, which was undoubtedly already sunk beyond reproach, and did not even hesitate. "Yes, let's. I like your friends, but they are somewhat—overwhelming. And besides, it's very hot, as young Lord George says."

"What, don't you like being the belle of the ball?" he asked quizzically as he led her out onto one of the blessedly cool terraces, strung under fairy lights. "I warned you you had become the heroine of the regiment."

She looked at the fairy lights and the presence of one of the big Spanish moons, all silver and beautiful, and knew that everything had indeed conspired against her. But there was a limit to how far even her badly overtaxed common sense would stretch. "Yes, it is remarkable how popular I have become. I fear it would quite go to my head if I weren't the only unattached Englishwoman in the room and probably the whole city," she retorted, grateful to feel the cool air on her overheated cheeks.

He laughed. "Not true. There are at least two other unattached Englishwomen in the room—both of them antidotes.

But I should know by now that Miss Alderstock finds some way of turning aside all compliments. You are a remarkable girl, my dear."

"No, merely a realistic one. And I am not a girl, you know. I was three-and-twenty on my last birthday. Quite an ape-leader, in fact."

"Yes, clearly past your last prayers—as evidenced by the clamoring court I just had to wrest you from. But I refuse to waste any more time talking about them. Tell me instead all that you have been doing since I saw you last."

"Indeed, there is little to tell," she said truthfully. "You know we reached Salamanca safely. I had anticipated no difficulty, and there was none."

"No," he said in amusement, "Prescott told me how you forded the Guardiana in spate. It might interest you to know I saw seasoned troopers washed away there. I looked for you in the town after we had entered it, hoping against hope that you might still be there. But I could learn nothing of any Englishwoman."

"No, Conchita was concerned for her father, so we didn't stay. Though I confess it was a bitter pill to swallow when we learned how quickly after we left the French had abandoned the town. But I am far more interested in hearing of your adventures. You had no trouble making it out of town? Father Gregorio found his mule the next day, and surmised you had gotten out safely."

"Oh, Lord yes. My horse was even where I had left him, fortunately with enough water and forage to last him, though he was a good deal disgruntled at having been abandoned for so long, I can tell you. I am indeed luckier than I deserve. After that I had little trouble in rejoining my regiment."

"Just in time to take part in all this marching, which can't have been good for you."

"Oh, I was in a capital way by then, thanks to your and Father Gregorio's excellent care," he said easily.

"And now the French have abandoned Madrid," she re-

marked a little dreamily. "I can still scarcely believe it. Seeing you march into Madrid more than made up for missing
Salamanca."

He grinned. "Yes, we are the heroes of the hour, which
makes a nice change. It would quite go to our heads, as you
say, if we were not as likely to be abused like pickpockets
when we march out again."

She was startled. "Will you? March out again?"

"I've no idea. But the French remain fixed in the north. I
should think we almost certainly will."

He sounded unconcerned, and she wondered what it was
like to be so secure in yourself as to know no fear. He was
leaning on the balcony at her side, handsome in his colorful
uniform, restored to health and vigor, already having taken
part in one major campaign and calmly prepared for any
number more, until he was killed or his goal was obtained.

She quickly closed her mind against that thought, but for
the first time it occurred to her that if the British army were
filled with such soldiers as Adam and his friends, the end of
the war was indeed inevitable. And if nothing else, she
could at least pride herself in having contributed a tiny part
to that victory through her rescue of this one man.

But that knowledge exacted its own heavy price. Foolish,
romantic dreams were one thing, but she had known for
some time now that she was somehow inextricably bound
up with this man in a way she little understood, and had
been from the moment she had seen him lying, stunned and
wounded, on that narrow street and had taken the fatal step
of intervening. Spanish legend had it you were forever responsible for the man whose life you saved, and she saw
now that it was true. If she had influenced his future by
saving his life—a statement that seemed unnecessarily
melodramatic to her, but was arguably true—then he had as
inexorably changed her own. From that moment, wherever
he went or whether or not they ever met again, she knew
that she would always think of him and wonder where he
was and what he was doing, and if he were alive or dead. It

was almost as if some invisible chain bound them together, surely an unforeseen result of her impulsive action.

As if he were thinking almost the same thing, he said quietly, "It almost seems a miracle to have found you like this. I have often thought of you in the last months, you know, wondering how you were faring, and whether you were safe. I've gone over at least a dozen times in my mind, the way you do, all the things I didn't say. I doubt I even thanked you properly, we parted in such a hurry, and I was scarcely in any shape to be thinking of anything. In fact I've cursed myself a hundred times for letting you go at all, for I should never have allowed you to talk me into such a dangerous risk. And now I have the opportunity, and I find myself as tongue-tied as ever. How do you thank someone for saving your life? Words seem completely inadequate."

She smiled a little in the dark. "And I was just thinking that you have already repaid me in a way I could never have anticipated. You have given me a stake in the battles. From now on, when I hear of a British victory against the French, I shall be able to say that in some small part I made it possible. Saving your life—if I did save it, which I'm not so convinced of—has had unexpected repercussions for both of us. Does that sound presumptuous? I fear it may."

To her relief he did not laugh at her, or make light of it. "I suspect you are vastly overrating my importance in any given battle," he said ruefully. "But I understand what you mean. I once saved a young ensign's life—a likable boy, but one I scarcely knew before that. I daresay I hadn't spoken a dozen words to him in my life. But by some trick of fate I was at the right spot to prevent him from being killed by a cannonball. I saw it coming, and in one of those instinctive decisions like the one that got me in so much trouble in Burgos, knocked him off his horse in time. The poor beast was killed instantly, but he was merely winded. After that, I felt the oddest proprietary interest in him. I wanted to know everything about him, and worried about him in battle."

"Yes, that's exactly it." Both of them were silent for a moment, then she asked quietly, "And what happened to him?"

He shrugged "He was later killed, during the assault at Ciudad Rodrigo."

She shivered despite herself, some of her fizzing happiness deflating a little. "I hope you will take better care of yourself," she made herself say lightly.

"That you can depend upon. But it goes both ways, you know. I am delighted to discover you safe in Madrid, but I would be even more delighted if you would take my advice and return to England. And before you say anything, let me finish. I know you have no relations there, but it has occurred to me that I have more than enough for both of us. You could easily go and live with my widowed mother, who would be delighted to have you, or one of my sisters, whose husband is also a soldier, and would be very happy for the company. I know your stubbornness by now, but believe me, things are going to get worse in Spain long before they get better. You would be much safer out of it. I wish I could take the time to escort you myself, but the devil's in it and I can't, for I must be off again almost at once. But I can easily arrange a military escort for you, and you could be home again in less than a month."

She was more than touched by his concern for her, and there was a part of her that wanted desperately to jump at the chance he offered. This night among his amusing friends had reminded her almost painfully of a part of her she had long forgotten, and roused an almost physical homesickness in her for familiar people and customs. More, surely if she were living with his relations, the chance of seeing him again and building upon what she felt shimmering to breathless life within her would be greater. At the very least she would be in a position to hear of him now and then, instead of facing the bleak wilderness of no news or contact at all once she returned home.

But it seemed moonbeams and folly could only go so far. And she had been more changed by that first fatal encounter than even she had yet suspected. What promise was implicit in his offer—or if he himself realized what might be made of it—she dared not allow herself to guess at. But another part of her recognized that what he offered was the very thing she most longed to escape: a safe life on the sidelines, waiting for him to come back—if he came back at all. The traditional woman's role. She would be condemned to the polite drawing rooms and stultifying if kindly concern of his relatives, in place of her stepfather's, and she would be even further away from the action.

Yes, he had made it more than plain he was of the school which protected its women and confined them in silken cages, however luxurious. And she was no longer sure that was enough for her. What she longed to do—had longed to do from the moment of meeting him—was to throw everything aside and go with him, sharing the camaraderie and hardship and the adventure. To follow the drum with him and leave behind all drawing rooms and safety. And that he had not offered.

She did not know when the stray ideas and thoughts percolating in her brain for so long had come to fruition, or when she had made up her mind, without being aware that that was what she was doing. But she saw now that her rescue of him that day had indeed changed her far more than even she had fully realized.

She lifted her head, as if to shake off her own thoughts, and said quietly, "And that is why I am not going to England, however grateful I may be for your kind offer. Nor am I remaining in Madrid in safety. I think it is more than time I stopped allowing the men in my life to keep all the adventure for themselves. And without appearing to boast, it has occurred to me that I am perhaps uniquely placed in all of Spain to help defeat the French."

Chapter 10

SHE HAD NOT expected to get by without an argument. Nor did she.

"You *what*?" he exploded.

"Only consider," she said calmly. "You yourself admitted Burgos would be a hard nut to crack without inside help. And since it is the center of Napoleon's communications, it obviously must be taken. I am even in the commandant's confidence. I can easily get information to you through Filipe. It would seem to me to be perfect."

He didn't even consider it. "No! It is completely out of the question!"

She was rather amused. "Anyway, it's not only that. You are infinitely kind—especially in offering the hospitality of your poor mother and sister. But aren't you forgetting my own adopted family?"

He appeared a little startled, then shrugged. "I think I had assumed, now that your sister is betrothed, that your responsibility would be at an end. Nor do they run the same risks as you do, for they are not English. But take them along. One of my sisters even resides in Bath, which might be the very thing for your ailing stepfather."

"You are more than generous—on your sisters' behalf. But only consider, my dear sir. Myself, an aging and bedridden invalid, a young girl and her duenna, all of whom are foreigners, not to mention the servants it would require to take care of my stepfather on the journey—that is quite an entourage to foist on some unsuspecting person, you must admit."

"No, why?" he demanded coolly. "Good God, you don't know my sisters. They are used to entertaining in the grand style. They would think nothing of so small a party, believe me."

"Even so, it is out of the question. Don Ottavio is far too ill to travel—indeed, I fear it would kill him! As for Conchita, she has just become betrothed, and I fancy her fiancé would have something to say about that."

"Then it becomes simpler. Leave them behind. I keep telling you they are not in the same danger as you are. You can return after the war is over, if you are still of a mind to. But keep in mind it has been a very long time since you saw England."

She wondered if he was always so ruthless, and shivered a little. He misunderstood the reason for it, and said abruptly, "You're cold. Shall I fetch a shawl for you?"

"No, indeed, it would be impossible to be cold on such a warm night. Unlike England, even in the summer. I do remember that."

Then, as the sound of someone approaching reached them, he swore in frustration. "Damnation! Look, this is too important to be discussed in such a place, and the devil's in it, I'm due to leave again tomorrow morning."

So much for moonbeams. Even she had not expected reality to return so quickly and with quite such a vengeance. But at least it proved she had been right to maintain her independence and pride. It was apt to be little enough to sustain her in the bitter coming months.

Pride made her keep her voice even so that she betrayed none of her pain to him. "I—see. You are leaving tomorrow? For how long?"

"Lord, I never know," he said impatiently. "A week—a month. That's why it seemed so miraculous that we ran into each other tonight, for I might have missed you completely. I think now it must have been meant, for I've got to talk you out of this folly. Look, I know Spanish families are devilish strict, but I'm taking you home. Stay here, and I'll go and get your shawl and warn your sister where you're going. Luckily I've a carriage waiting for me, since I planned to leave early in any case. Don't run away, and don't let any of my so-called friends steal you away. In fact, if it's not too cold for you, come and sit on one of these benches in the garden, where no one will find you. I'll be back as quickly as I can."

She was content enough to wait for him, coming to terms with the bitter dregs of her foolish flight into fantasy. As for being cold, it was but another of the absurd myths perpetuated by men: that women were but delicate creatures to be protected from the least draft, even in the middle of a hot summer. The air was warm and fragrant, perfumed with a thousand blossoms. And the traitorous moon was overhead still, as if fairy tales were still possible, and the cold dawn when he would be gone again did not lie only a few hours away.

She wondered idly what Conchita would find to tell her fiancé's relations, and if she would have a shred of reputation left to her in the morning. At the moment it did not seem to matter overmuch. And it was doubtless one of the things she would have to jettison if she meant to cease being content with a woman's passive role in life.

The major was as good as his word, and returned very quickly, bearing her shawl, which he insisted upon putting about her shoulders, and then conducting her in a roundabout way to the front carriage drive with a skill that spoke of long experience in circumventing duennas.

Besides, it was clearly time to get things back on a less personal basis, and so she said teasingly, "I am impressed by your staff work, by the way. Had you this exit planned in hopes of a lovely Madrilenian? Certainly the manner in which you whisked me away spoke of a great deal of practice."

"But then it is the Hussar motto to be prepared in all circumstances," he countered audaciously. "Here is my carriage. Mind your step."

Reggie allowed him to hand her up and tuck a light rug across her lap, reflecting ruefully that despite her new resolve it was nice to be coddled and treated as fine porcelain once in a while.

He settled himself beside her and said abruptly, "I have ordered the driver to go a little way out of town instead of taking you directly home. There is a promontory that gives a good view of the city, and where we will be uninterrupted. And I really must talk to you."

She made herself laugh and guessed, "And besides, you need to reconnoiter it? Very well. I may as well be hung for a sheep as a lamb, since it would seem I have thrown discretion out the window."

It was his turn to laugh, if ruefully. "Unkind! I have already reconnoitered it. How else do you think I knew it was there? Wellington always likes to scout out the heights in any position. I have ridden every mile of the area, I promise you."

But he did not seem to agree with her that a lighter note was called for, for he added rather impatiently, "But enough of this nonsense. Let us deal rather with your far more dangerous nonsense. My dear girl, it would be madness to return to Burgos—especially at this time."

She eyed him sharply. "Ah, Wellington does mean to attack it then?" They had begun to leave the lights of the town behind, and it was very pleasant out in the warm darkness. The moon, her avowed enemy by now, showed them the way, and shed its light over everything, turning even mundane buildings and objects into unexpectedly magical mysteries as if to taunt her.

He made an impatient gesture. "I am not privy to his plans. But I can assure you that the situation will be getting much worse in that area before it gets better. You run the very real risk of finding yourself in the middle of a pitched battle, or even a siege, which is far worse. And if that happens, the French may belatedly remember you are English, and your position could become more than dangerous."

"I see. And so I am to turn tail and run? It seems to me that if the army were to follow your advice, we would have no hope of defeating the French."

"Then you little understand the art of defense, my girl. Even Wellington knows when to advance and when it is time for an expeditious retreat. I would prefer to have you safe in England again, and hope I may persuade you of that. But in any case, to return to Burgos would be nothing short of madness."

"Why? Because I am a woman?"

"I would advise the same to a man in such dangerous circumstances. Don't forget, you are an enemy there, however little anyone may have recalled the fact to date. But yes, it certainly doesn't help matters that you are a woman."

"And women are to be protected from the harsher aspects of war? My dear sir, do you imagine I think it some pleasant contest between rival teams? If so you are mistaken. I sometimes think in fact that it is only men who truly romanticize war. Women know too much of its outcome."

"Good Lord! What next will you say?" he exclaimed in exasperation.

"It's the truth. You and your friends laughed and joked of a very bloody campaign just now in my hearing. How many men did you lose personally? And how many friends? No, it is not women who romanticize war. All of those men had grieving wives or sisters or mothers, who knew nothing or even cared of its strategic importance, or the ultimate outcome. They can only mourn, while those of you still alive soon forget that battle and those fallen comrades in the next and then the next. It seems to me you men have indeed been most selfish in keeping all the glory to yourselves. You talk of being safely out of the war, but you and your friends would sooner die than return to England before the end is reached. That much was clear from your talk. Well, I have recently discovered I am not so very different. I am tired of the portion stingily allotted to women, of waiting and grieving when the time comes, with no part in the adventure."

"Good God! It seems to me you have had a large part in the adventure already. Too large a part for my peace of mind. I would see you safely under my mother's wing."

Thus spoke the traditional male arrogance. And she was sufficiently feminine to weaken a little under all that flattering male protectiveness. It was something she would have to guard against, it seemed.

"I see. War and battle and heroics are reserved to men. We poor women must be content to make do with our portion of grief and waiting."

He was frowning heavily in the dark. "If that sounds hard, I apologize for it. But you are the ones who hold civilization together, my dear, and we instinctively know it. No, I don't mean to be patronizing. But you have grown up in a harsh crucible. Is it wrong to want to see you escape from all this, to laugh and dance as you did tonight? No, let me finish. Several things you have said, both tonight and before, make me think you believe yourself on the shelf, or past your last prayers. But that is complete nonsense—although you are indeed right that a Spanish husband would never do for you. Go to England, and let my sister introduce you to some eligible men. Believe me, she would like nothing better."

She took a deep breath. So, it had been said. What he offered was no more than the concern of any kind gentleman, not promises for the future. She had been a fool to expect more. She saw without much surprise that it was clouding up, as if even the moon had at last abandoned the unequal contest. Certainly the intoxication of moonbeams had long since worn off. Now she was merely cold and disillusioned, and more than a little angry. "I am to turn my thoughts to the more suitable ones of husbands and children. Is that it? And you insist you don't mean to be patronizing?"

He swore again. "If that is patronizing, I don't apologize for it. And you are indeed naive if you believe your sex makes no difference. I have no desire to frighten you, but perhaps it is time someone did. After the sieges of Badajoz and Ciudad Rodrigo conditions were worse than you can begin to imagine, I thank God. No women were safe, not even nuns—and these were British troops, not the French, mind you. Is that brutal enough for you? Our officers could do nothing to control them, and had to stand by and let the debauchery run its course, or else risk being shot by our own men. I should not be saying such things to you, except that you are a sensible woman, and I've no time to mince words. Now do you begin to understand?"

"Yes," she said, despite herself feeling a little sick. "We had heard—but I didn't wish to believe it."

"And I don't like talking of it. But I warned you that you little realized the realities of war. And whether or not you like to be obliged to acknowledge them, they are different for women than for men."

But she had pulled herself back together again. "Perhaps. But now that you have warned me, I shall take care to have some means of taking my own life if it should become necessary," she retorted. "But that isn't what you mean, of course. You mean I should give up the entire notion and remember I am a mere female, and thus too weak and inconsequential to ever make anything change."

"No! Damn it, that is not what I mean."

"Then perhaps you could explain to me why you are allowed to take risks, but I am not?"

He hesitated, then as if goaded, said, "Then perhaps this will explain it to you," and he abruptly pulled her into his arms and kissed her.

As a kiss it was a fairly shattering affair, and showed her that it did not require the presence of moonlight to throw her completely out of her shaky calm. He had kissed her before, but that gentle salute bore no relation to this one, for he was frustrated and angry, and quite clearly took it out on her. But even so it was enough to set her pulse to hammering and all the blood rushing giddily to her head so that she feared she would faint for the first time in her life.

When he at last released her, she sat up, shaken and bruised and more angry than she could remember being, and could not have found her voice if she had tried to.

He sat with his back to her in the narrow coach, breathing hard as well. "I'm sorry!" he said harshly after a moment. "I didn't mean that to happen."

She was having a good bit of trouble with her own breathing. But she said dangerously, "Didn't you?"

He turned back to her quickly at that, very little of the amiable, charming man she knew still in evidence. "And what in sweet Christ is that supposed to mean?"

"There is no need to swear at me! Or are you trying to prove that that, too, is something I shall have to learn to cope with, as well as being manhandled, if I do as I intend?"

Her voice shook a little, and she realized the scene was rapidly getting out of hand. So much for moonbeams indeed. "Or didn't you kiss me in the hopes that if all other arguments failed, you might persuade me that way? Isn't that the ultimate and classical male answer? A few easy kisses, to remind me of my inescapable role in life, and I should no doubt be happy to abandon my principles and wait patiently for you to condescend to return to me—if you return at all, and don't die on one of your dangerous missions. But even then I should no doubt be satisfied to have fulfilled my ultimate destiny, and sacrificed my happiness on the altar of male conceit. Isn't that it?"

He swore again and abruptly thrust open the door and jumped out of the carriage, striding angrily away in the dark.

She waited for a long minute, then climbed out after him, ridiculously annoyed to find the task an awkward one without the steps having been let down. For the first time that evening she cursed her absurd finery, designed with no other purpose in mind than to please the very male she was now defying. It seemed her biology was determined to defeat her, but she was equally determined not to let it.

When she reached him he said colorlessly, without turning, "I apologize. You may be right."

She was unprepared for the apology and taken a little aback. "That—is generous of you," she conceded reluctantly. "And I apologize as well. It would seem we both let things get slightly out of hand."

He still did not turn back to face her. "I apologize for kissing you at that time and in that way. Perhaps I did mean it as a species of polite blackmail. But I don't apologize for kissing you. I have wanted to do it almost from the first moment I laid eyes on you, as you know very well. Perhaps you will agree that gives me some right to concern myself with your future?"

That was a decidedly low blow. She saw that in any battle with this man she would have to be very much on her guard. "How am I to know very well?" she countered irritably. "A moment ago you were calmly plotting my marriage to some unknown Englishman! Anyway, does that same truth give me the right to object to your own actions?"

He turned at last. "I don't know. Yes. No. I will confess my objections have a great deal to do with my feelings toward you and the danger you would be running. As for what is between us, don't pretend you aren't as aware of it as I am. If I was plotting your marriage to an Englishman, it was because I am trying to retain what little sense I seem to have left. But the difference between us is that I am a soldier, and as such was trained to danger and knew what I was doing when I joined up. It is not the same at all for you, and I know of no man alive who would not feel the same. I will grant you all the bravery and patriotism that you desire, my dear. How could I do anything less, when I owe my life to you, and the information you succeeded in getting through may very well have turned the battle in our favor? But can't you be content with that? You are the most

remarkable woman I know. But I won't apologize for wishing to see you safely out of the war now. If that is selfish
I'm sorry for it."

"And that is where it ultimately ends," she said bitterly.
"I saved your life and so you must be grateful to me. The
truth is, we have been thrown together under . . . rather dramatic circumstances, and it would be foolish for either of
us to trust them."

He was silent for a long moment. Then he shrugged and
said ruefully, "God knows I never meant to say any of this.
I have no right to. Whatever there is between us, and I am
the last to profess to know what that is, I am in no position
to make you any promises, or ask you to wait for me. I may
well be dead tomorrow. I have nothing to offer you but fear
and uncertainty, and I would be a blackguard to tie you to
me under the circumstances—however much I might like
to. But right or wrong, in the end I keep coming back to
this!"

And he took her roughly in his arms and again kissed
her.

Chapter 11

THIS TIME IT was very different. If his kiss before had been a fairly shattering affair, then he had been angry and bent on punishing her. Now Reggie had time to reflect ruefully—while she still had any wits left to think at all—that Major Adam Canfield had far too much experience in convincing females to abandon all resistance.

He was again the first to draw back, saying raggedly, "God! I'm sorry. I shouldn't have done that, for my sake as well as yours. And the devil's in it, I have no power to compel you to be sensible. But is there nothing I can say to convince you that what you are proposing is madness?"

She had no wish for him to discover just how weak she was at that particular moment. It was clear he had far more experience with this sort of thing than she did, and every word he said seemed designed to pit her frail strength against herself. But then, for all his experience with her sex, she thought he little understood the feminine heart. She had been tied to him long since with bonds far stronger than frail promises.

But at least he had made his position more than clear. He was clearly attracted to her, but determined to make no promises. She said dryly, "And yet you would demand certainties of me. It would seem your position is a trifle inconsistent."

"Perhaps," he conceded raggedly. "You are right that war is cruelest on the women forced to wait at home. If that's inconsistent, I'm sorry for it. But I have seen too many widows made already to want to add another to the list."

She dared to say softly, "And yet not all wives wait at home."

He rejected that immediately, as she had already known he would. "Good God! Perhaps we men do keep all the fun for ourselves, but the army is no place for a woman. I know there are a number of well-bred women who follow the drum. But it is impossible for everyone concerned. The women live uncomfortable, irregular lives, poor wretches, separated from their husbands for long stretches of time and forever worried about them; and the poor devils they are married to forever after find themselves torn between their duties and their wives, a cleft stick that has no solution. I have seen too many good officers ruined by bringing their wives out with them to ever want to add to their ranks, believe me. More, the presence of such camp followers is a constant nuisance, playing havoc with logistics and supplies and influencing the outcome of more campaigns than you might believe possible. I know Wellington is famed for cursing their existence and has frequently threatened to banish all women completely. If you don't like that, I'm sorry, but it is the unfortunate truth."

And that was that. He demanded of her what he was not willing to give himself, and she could either choose to be packed off like so much unwanted baggage, in hopes that he would survive the war and return in the same mind he was in now, and had not in the meantime fallen madly in love with some charming señorita. Or she could maintain her own independence, at whatever cost to herself and her dreams.

And in the end there was no real choice, of course. Moonbeams were very well in their place, but the cold dawn always came with its harsh realities, however willfully you pulled the covers over your head.

After a long moment she said drearily, "Perhaps you're right, and only frankness will serve now. I, too, am—aware of some link between us, that much must be obvious. But I certainly expect neither marriage nor promises from you. And that being the case, it seems to me that you deny me the one right you reserve so jealously for yourself. You do not hesitate to place your duty above everything else—even your own safety. But you would deny me the same right."

He almost groaned. "It seems I should have learned from my first encounter with you! You are right, I have absolutely no right to demand of you what I cannot give myself. And yet, what you propose is madness."

"Is it? It sounds pompous to say it is my duty, as much as yours is, but it's how I feel. How can I turn my back on that merely because I run a little danger? Especially when men like you and Filipe and all those other pleasant young men I laughed and danced with tonight are risking your lives every day to defend what I hold as dear as you do?"

She shivered, and he said almost accusingly, "You are cold! Here, take my pelisse."

He insisted upon enfolding her in his pelisse with all its gay silver lacing and oddly reassuring odors of tobacco and cologne. She knew it was not the cold that had made her shiver, but she huddled into it gratefully.

"Why is it that what you feel most deeply always sounds the most unforgivable when you put it in words?" she asked lightly. "That's the curse of the English, I suppose, and I have just discovered recently how very English I am. But I have also discovered I would far rather live with my conscience than in safety, and it seems I can't do both. You, if anyone, must understand that."

After a long moment he said unwillingly, "I think I always knew I must lose this particular argument. It would seem we are more alike than I knew. Very well. But at least give me your word you won't run any unnecessary risks."

"Certainly—if you give me the same."

He laughed, and dropped his arm rather tightly around her shoulders. "I begin to think you are tougher than I gave you credit for. You have certainly rompéd me. Perhaps if I did not have to go tomorrow I might hope to wear you down. But it would seem we are fated to keep on meeting and be torn apart."

"Yes," she said and shivered again despite the warm weight of his arm, which instantly tightened still more about her. "You will be—careful, won't you?"

She could see him grinning in the dark. "I've taken precious good care of my skin so far. I wish I might feel as confident about you."

"You may," she told him truthfully. "Believe me, my days are far more filled with tedium than adventure. I am envious of your freedom and your cause, since I am myself handicapped by my petticoats and must be content to experience only the fringes of the real excitement. You don't know how lucky you are."

She thought he dropped a quick kiss on her hair, though she could not be sure. "I am beginning to," he said cryptically. "But I must get you back. I fear it is very late."

"And you must be on your way."

He hesitated, then shrugged. "There is that, too. I wish— but it does no good. Duty is duty, as you so rightly point out. It would seem ours continues to separate us at the most inconvenient of times."

She agreed, but thought it was perhaps as well they were to be separated. She was not at all sure her willpower or her resolution would long survive a prolonged siege by Major Adam Canfield.

Neither of them said much more, but then there was little enough to say. For her part, Reggie was having to strongly remind herself how foolish it was to long to cling to moonbeams, when she might never see this man again, and he might very well be dead all too terrifyingly soon. It seemed far more dangerous to her in that moment than the mere passing on of military secrets.

As dangerous as it was to read more into the situation than he obviously intended. He had been careful to give her no promises, and she would be a fool to see in his words, or in his kisses, anything but what they undoubtedly were: the overheated feelings of two strangers passing in the night and clinging to each other for comfort.

She fully expected the cold rain that began to fall as they drove back to town. It was somehow more than fitting.

Reggie and Conchita returned to Burgos two weeks later. During that time there had been no further word from Major Canfield. Presumably he was still out on his mission, whatever that was, and she could only pray he was safe, and not lying anonymously dead in some field or languishing in a French prison.

At any rate, having so pompously asserted her independence and determination to fulfill her duty, she supposed somewhat ruefully that she now had no choice but to live up to her boasting.

In truth, she could not have done anything else. It was unthinkable to drag poor Conchita and Don Ottavio to London with her—and equally unthinkable to leave them behind. Even to remain in Madrid posed insoluble difficulties—and they had no guarantee that the British would remain there anyway, as Adam had said.

But if it had been hard to return to Burgos and its French garrison before, it was proving doubly hard now. Then she had had but a taste of being among her own people again. This time, she had enjoyed nearly two weeks of it, for if the major was absent, his friends and the other officers she had met, either at the ball or in camp, were not slow to pursue the acquaintance. Starting early the next morning they called on the slimmest of pretexts or no pretext at all, inundated her with invitations to attend picnics, teas, or the parading of troops, and vied with each other to amuse her.

It was all very flattering, and had she not been fully aware of the reason for this attention it might indeed have gone to her head. As it was, she laughed at their lighthearted nonsense, liked them all very much, and knew that it would only make it that much harder, when the time came, to return to the alien life she had, until recently, taken so very much for granted.

As for Major Canfield, it was wisest not to think of him at all. And if she found herself valuing her new friends as much because they knew him and frequently talked of him as for their own sakes, that was something she kept very much to herself.

The return trip was tedious and uncomfortable, closed up as they were in an airless coach in the sweltering August heat. And it was oddly dispiriting to pass from British hands to the familiar and now-despised French troops. With King Joseph now in the north, they were more in evidence than ever, and she had reason once again to be grateful for Monsieur de Thierry's passport.

Once home again, life soon regained an unpleasantly familiar routine, as if those days in Madrid had never been. Nor, despite all her renewed hopes, were the French in the town by any means pessisimistic about the immediate future of the war. Lord Wellington, recently made a marquis, so rumor went, by a belatedly grateful English Parliament, might have taken Ciudad Rodrigo and Badajoz by siege, driven the French out of Salamanca, and marched triumphantly into the capital. But the French army in Spain was still some two hundred thousand strong, nearly four times Wellington's strength, and word had come that Napoleon had taken Smolensk and was sweeping victoriously on through Russia. Perhaps more important to the immediate future of Spain, America had declared war on Britain, with direct consequences on the Peninsular campaign. The mouth of the Channel and the coasts of Portugal would now swarm with American privateers, which fact could only work to the advantage of the French, for until now Wellington had had it all his own way in the matter of shipping and thus transport and supply of his troops.

It was sobering enough news, reminding Reggie that those heady days in Madrid had indeed been a time out of reality. And reminding her as well, if she had needed it, that nothing could matter until the French had been driven completely out of Spain.

And though it was difficult to bite her tongue and listen to such talk, it was sometimes surprising what stray tidbits of news she was able to pick up in that way, details let slip during the course of a convivial evening, and which she duly passed on to Filipe when he came.

Even thinking of her stepbrother made Reggie smile. Filipe was as volatile and rash as his sister Conchita was gentle. He hated the French with all the concentrated hatred of one in whose veins ran the purest Castilian blood, and on the rare occasions he returned for a formal visit—he slipped in many times informally, for he had devised his own means of hoodwinking the French guards—he could scarcely be brought to be polite to them, when his safety and far too often even his life depended upon biting his tongue.

He was ostensibly at university in Madrid, but had for some years been with the guerillas in the north under Julian Sanchez. These, as the major had conceded, were frequently of far more use to the Allied cause than the regular Spanish troops, far too often commanded by aging and generally incompetent generals. According to Felipe the guerillas could be relied upon to harass the enemy rear whenever the French were on the move, to the fury of the French marshals frequently capturing a goodly number of men and cannon. They also took pleasure in relieving the French of as many supplies as they could, and made it one of their chief goals to interfere wherever possible with their communications.

In fact there had been a time a few years ago, according to Filipe, when they had so effectively intercepted every messenger to the French emperor that Massena had had to send an emissary with a guard of six hundred men he could ill afford to spare in order to get his information through. It was but another instance of the French arrogance and stupidity, also according to Filipe, that Napoleon continued to direct affairs in Spain from a thousand miles away, with no understanding of the country or the people, and when conditions had too often changed completely by the time he could get an order through.

They had been home but a short time when news was received that Wellington was at last marching on Burgos. Filipe confirmed it when he slipped into town the next night. He was a dark, handsome youth, lounging on the edge of her bed in his colorful clothes, looking to her mind scarcely old enough to be risking his life every day so recklessly. He had wakened her out of a sound sleep, but she was so used to him appearing and then disappearing like a wraith that she seldom even started to find him shaking her awake at some dark hour and urging her laughingly not to sleep the night away.

He received the news of her recent adventures and new plans with amusement, but did not disappoint her by suggesting she had been foolish to involve herself, or that she should not have risked his sister. He, too, knew all too well the importance of valid information.

In answer to her question he admitted that Wellington was indeed intending to besiege Burgos—though he doubted he would succeed. "For I'll give them this, your squabbling French marshals!—they dare not give it up as easily as they did Salamanca if they value their heads. Napoleon is not noted for tolerating the mistakes of others, though he makes far more serious ones himself, to my mind. *Madre de Dios!* He has yet to see the danger of Wellington, even after all this. He believes all the French newspapers who hope to flatter him by calling him the 'Sepoy General' and dismissing his genius. Well, they shall soon enough find out what this 'Sepoy General' is capable of. To top it off, Napoleon has even taken some of the most seasoned troops from Spain for this foolish Russian venture of his."

Then he grinned. "Not that I have any reason to complain! Add to that the fact that Marmont and Soult and the puppet Joseph quarrel among themselves endlessly, and waste any chance they might have had of uniting to defeat Wellington, and they do everything but hand us Spain back on a silver platter. I should know, for we intercept enough of their messages! And amusing some of them are, too. The fools! They need not have given up Salamanca if they had been able to cease their jealous sniping long enough to heed the warnings they had. Oh, it makes us laugh, but they are none of them fit to be in command. And Napoleon sends them useless orders that are either out of date or wholly misunderstands the terrain they must fight over, since he has never seen the country, and then he expects them to be obeyed to the letter! I tell you they deserve to be beaten, and they will be, soon enough, God willing."

Conchita came in then, in her wrapper and yawning sleepily, her dark hair in a braid down her back. She hugged her brother warmly and curled up at his side, retaining his hand in her much smaller one. They were much alike in looks, if not in temperament, for Conchita was sweet and uncomplicated, and tended to be placid, while Filipe was fiery and volatile, quick to laughter as well as anger.

She scolded him for curling on Reggie's bed in all his dirt. "For I must tell you, my brother, that you need a bath!" she pointed out frankly.

"I know I do. Only there's no time tonight. I must be gone before dawn. They've tightened the guard recently. But what of you, my sister?" he teased her. "You've become a heroine since last I saw you, I hear. Reggie has been telling me of your adventures."

"Oh, no, that is all Reggie," she said placidly. "I did nothing."

"On the contrary." Reggie was rueful. "I fear if anything had gone wrong, you would have suffered as well as I."

"No, no, for you are too clever," Conchita assured her. "At any rate, *de nada*. It is my country you try to defend, after all. Now tell us, Filipe, all that has happened to you since last we saw you. But first you must eat."

"No, I'm not hungry. We are all eating high on the hog, for we were able to liberate a French baggage train not long ago. But I will take some wine back with me. And some more medical supplies. I hope you have them for me?"

Reggie nodded, and satisfied, he told them several amusing, and too often hair-raising tales. Conchita listened serenely to it all, though once or twice her hand tightened rather spasmodically on his.

But too soon for her satisfaction he pulled himself up off the bed, saying he must be off. He only paused to ask, "And Father? How is he?"

"Oh, he is so much better," Conchita assured him optimistically. "He was able to eat almost the whole of his dinner, and was sleeping soundly when I left him."

Filiple cast a look at Reggie over his sister's head, and frowned as she shook her own slightly. Both knew that Don Ottavio was unlikely to recover fully, if at all, and would probably be an invalid for the rest of his life.

Filipe looked grim for a moment, then shrugged and shook it off. He had one or two messages for Reggie to pass on to his compatriots in the north. These tended to be well-born young men like himself, used to every luxury, and yet who had voluntarily given up their easy lives and educations to go and live in the hills like savages and fight for their country. They inspired Reggie to continue to fight for her adopted country, even when she was most pessimistic about the chances of ever defeating the French.

She had been in the habit for some time of being a sort of informal liaison between the various guerilla groups. Sometimes she rode out of the town, ostensibly for exercise, and would, seemingly by accident, meet a shabby young man on horseback, or on foot, and pass on a few quick words.

Or sometimes they would slip into town, like Filipe, and use the small hidden side door always kept unlatched, usually wolfing down a meal while she gave them any messages she had, and as frequently raiding the larder before they left again, while massive Maria looked impassively on without a word as Sunday's dinner was packed up and rapidly vanished.

This time Reggie was able to tell Filipe one or two snippets that might be important to the British, if they did indeed mean to attack the town. Filipe promised to see they got passed on, and while Conchita went away to fetch him a few things she was convinced he required for his comfort, he said abruptly, "Your major was right. If the British do besiege the town, it could be dangerous. Nor, even if they fail, are you likely to find it pleasant. Perhaps you should have stayed in Madrid."

She let the reference to "her" major pass, and asked calmly, "And leave Conchita to take care of everything here? In fact, I will send her back if you feel it is safer."

He shrugged. "I doubt if she'd go. She is amazingly docile until she makes up her mind to something, then like all women, she can be remarkably stubborn. But it is likely to be even more uncomfortable for you, being a foreigner here."

"Luckily, not even the French seem to remember very often that I am English," she told him cheerfully, dismissing the problem.

Much later she was to remember those lighthearted words with a certain amused bitterness at her own naivete.

Chapter 12

FILIPE'S NEWS of a possible British invasion was soon common knowledge, and it engendered considerable panic in the town among its Spanish inhabitants. Most, however, threw up their hands in resignation and doubted whether it would matter much to them in the long run. Whether it was French or English in dominance over them made little odds, for few by now believed their country's independence would be restored to them. For twenty years they had endured French rule, and there were children now who did not even remember the time when Spain had her own king and could hold up her head in the world.

Reggie, busy gathering necessary supplies to withstand a possible siege, and learning all she could from her French connections, joined them in hardly knowing whether to hope for a British attack or not. She could not forget what Adam had told her of the sieges at Ciudad Rodrigo and Badajoz, and her own eyes and common sense told her the French would not give up Burgos without a desperate struggle.

Somewhat to her secret shame, Monsieur de Thierry, the French commandant, proved more than helpful. He informed Reggie and Conchita, in strictest confidence, that the rumors of possible invasion were true, but that she and her charming sister had no need to panic. Burgos was invincible and Wellington had not the men to take it. Nor would the town ever be surrendered, as Salamanca was, for the emperor himself had ordered it defended to the last man. Besides, the British general was sending but a portion of his troops against the town, a curious omission that merely demonstrated his incompetence and guaranteed the failure of his current expedition.

Reggie pumped him as much as she dared on the town's preparations, under the guise of being worried for her own and her stepsister's safety, and did not find his answers as reassuring as he so obviously intended. It did indeed seem as if Burgos was impregnable, and she dreaded the loss of men if Wellington invested the town and failed to reduce it.

But in the event the commandant had some even more startling news than the threat of invasion. He had received word in their absence that his wife had died. He was now a widower.

Upon their conventional expressions of condolence, he spread his hands. He was a middle-aged man of medium height and a not inconsiderable Gallic charm. "Ah, thank you *mesdemoiselles*. It is like your kind hearts. But you must understand that it has been nearly four years since I have seen my wife. It is sad, *quelle triste, en effet,* but what would you? One forgets, and life must go on."

Conchita, who spoke French as fluently as Reggie herself did, said everything that was proper, but she could not help casting a slightly mischievous glance at Reggie. Thankfully, however, Monsieur de Thierry did not remain much longer, only assuring them as he left that if he foresaw the least danger he would send word to warn them and would not hesitate to extend to them his own protection.

He pressed Reggie's hand somewhat more warmly than strict decorum dictated on parting and promised to do himself the honor of calling again when the pressures of work permitted.

It was a development that Conchita could not forebear to tease her about. She insisted that her dearest Reggie would undoubtedly soon receive an offer from the French commandant, for there could now be no doubt that he had developed a pronounced *tendre* for her. It only remained to be seen how long he would allow decorum to overcome his ardor, and make her an open declaration.

But for once Reggie failed to be amused by her nonsense. It was a complication she could well have done without, for if true, she faced a difficult task of keeping the commandant at arm's length while not discouraging his visits—and thus his flow of information. Even more daunting, her own position as a foreigner might not be so secure without his goodwill and protection. In fact, she could have cursed his poor unfortunate and ungrieved wife for dying at such an inconvenient moment.

For it was true she dared not lightly discard the commandant's friendship. She had little doubt it was his doing that they had not had French troops quartered on them, or their house seized entirely for the use of some French officer or dignitary, which would have been inconvenient, to say the least, for her stepbrother's movement.

Although she was able to pass on Monsieur de Thierry's assessments of the proposed siege to Filipe fairly soon, she had no way of knowing whether it actually reached the British or not, of course. At any rate, on September 19th the British did indeed besiege Burgos.

It was a situation that immediately put Reggie under a particularly draining conflict of emotions, for try as she might she could not put out of her mind that it was her own countrymen camped just outside the gates. It was all the more unreal to her to know that among them might very well be some of the men she had danced and laughed with that night in Madrid.

She did her best to discover what British regiments were involved, without much success. It was even more ironic to think that Adam might even at that moment be within a quarter of a mile from her, and she would never know it. The town swarmed with French soldiers, and security was so tight that not even Filipe dared risk trying to get in.

But life under siege proved very little different from usual, at least at first. The town was well supplied, though some rationing was ordered, and none of the citizens were in any immediate danger. It was the constant and murderous firing from the walls down into the British mines and trenches, and the booming of the British and Portuguese cannon in return that wore badly on the nerves of everyone. Day after day the noise dragged on, with no visible change or indication of how the siege was going.

And as the days passed, the Spanish inhabitants of the town cursed the French and British equally, and tended to remain indoors as much as possible. There were days when the fearful cannonade would stop only for a few hours at night; and even then it seemed to echo in one's head, so that the brief hours of peace were little help. Reggie, lying wakeful night after night, and trying not to think of the British lives it might be costing, discovered that those brief hours of respite were almost worse than the noise. It was even worse to lie there dreading its starting up again at dawn, and imagining the exhausted British troops snatching a few hours of sleep before launching the attack again, or returning to the digging of their mines.

Certainly she did not need to see the murderous fire poured down day after day from the walls into the British lines to know what dreadful slaughter was going on. But once Monsieur de Thierry arranged for her to be on the ramparts at daybreak, to see for herself the sight of the British army drawn up before the walls of the town. It was one of the more trying moments in her newfound calling, for the sight moved her unbearably, and she had had to turn away quickly to hide the film of tears, before being able to congratulate the commandant on the excellence of his defenses.

She grew thinner, and lost a good deal of her usual blooming color, but at least there was work to do, and Conchita and Don Ottavio to comfort. Conchita, possessing far more feminine sensibility than Reggie, had a tendency to start even at ordinary sounds. The constant bombardment had her nerves frayed almost past bearing, so that she was in genuine danger of making herself ill. Don Ottavio as well, frail and bedridden, suffered almost as much from knowing his country was in need, and he could do nothing but lie there, in the constant noise, weak and helpless.

When Reggie discovered he had insisted his servant drag out his sword and leave it at his bedside, in case of need, she was moved almost to tears. The idea of what he could do to protect them in his frail state was ludicrous, but to comfort him she showed him her own pistol, supplied to her by Filipe on one of his now-curtailed nocturnal visits. She had practiced with it until she could handle and fire it with ease. It had been captured from the French on one of the guerilla raids, and had evidently been fashioned for a lady's hand, as an amusing trinket, for it looked little more than a toy, tiny and chased with silver. But Filipe assured her it could put a hole in a man at twenty paces, and in those days she slept with it under her pillow, and never went out without it. She had not forgotten Adam's dire warnings, and had every intention of using it in defense of herself and Conchita if it should become necessary.

That reassured Don Ottavio slightly, but it was a terrible time for all of them. The servants were edgy and had to be continually reassured, the constant noise of the cannon wore on all their nerves, and the heat was such that it was difficult to sleep even in the brief blessed hours of silence granted to them. And as the days and weeks of the siege wore on, Reggie had to reflect with some bitterness how lightly she had boasted she might help turn the tide of the war in favor of the British.

For now that the time for heroics had arrived, she could think of little she could do to help her country. Adam had told her the art of war lay in knowing when to fight and when to retreat, but she could not escape the unwelcome suspicion that the frailty of her sex had somehow defeated her. More than anything, she discovered, she longed to be outside the town with her countrymen, fighting and perhaps laying down her life in a noble cause, instead of being penned up there, forced to come to terms with her own impotence.

Monsieur de Thierry found time once or twice to call and reassure Reggie on the success of the town's resistance and the ultimate futility of the English assault, wholly unaware of the irony in such reassurance. Each time he brought her some delicacy imported from France that he hoped she and her so charming sister might make use of. As she could see, the British stood no chance of succeeding in their blockade so long as supplies could still get through so easily. He had said all along that Wellington's victories had been overrated, the result of lucky circumstance, not superior tactical ability.

Such times it was all Reggie could do to bite her tongue and thank him for his thoughtfulness. She would then pass on whatever he gave her promptly to Father Gregorio to give to some deserving parishioners. It was a fine and gratifying display of pride, but she knew she dare not indulge herself in such displays too often. For many reasons, including her stepsister's and stepfather's safety, she could not afford to offend the French commandant. If she were to be unable to smile and meet with the enemy without giving her growing hatred away, she would be of no use to anyone. It would seem the life she had chosen was more difficult even than she had anticipated; but if Adam and Filipe could do it, she was determined she could, too.

Then, without warning, on the morning of October 20th the British lifted the siege and retreated. The silence alerted her first, as the citizens of the town emerged like turtles from their houses to test the air. Rumor soon spread that the British had withdrawn in the night watches as silently as they had arrived, and their abandoned tunnels and breastworks soon bore mute witness to the truth of this statement. In place of the colorful army camped before the walls for a month, nothing remained but the scars in the countryside, and the sometimes still-smouldering campfires of the departed army.

Monsieur de Thierry paid Reggie a congratulatory call and informed her with some smugness that it had merely been a matter of time before the British general realized the overwhelming odds he was facing and withdrew. The French army, reorganized and consolidated, could now boast a concentration of one hundred ten thousand seasoned French troops against Lord Wellington's eighty thousand, twenty-five thousand of whom were uncertain Spanish allies. The French army was even now in hot pursuit and Monsieur de Thierry was in hourly expectation of hearing the enemy had been speedily overtaken and the whole army put to rout.

The British defeat was hard enough to bear, but Reggie was to discover that the silence was almost worse than the guns had been. Her heart was with the retreating British, and she lived in hourly dread of hearing they had indeed been badly beaten, or even defeated. Nor had she realized, during the long siege, what a comforting feeling it had been to her to know her countrymen were just outside the gates, until that last connection was withdrawn.

Not until word came that the British had retired to winter quarters in Portugal did she breathe a sigh of relief, tempered with the inevitable disappointment to know she was wholly on her own again. She wondered where Adam was and if he was safe, but it was obvious she faced a long winter and spring under French rule before she could even hope to see him again.

Then November brought two startling developments. Freed from his worries, Monsieur de Thierry came to make Reggie a formal proposal of marriage. And Adam used Filipe's route to slip into town.

The first of these events began innocently enough. The French commandant had called, as he had grown increasingly wont to do, and from Reggie's point of view it was mere bad luck that he found only herself at home, for once.

Conchita had gone out to visit a friend, and was not back yet.

Monsieur de Thierry accepted her explanations with a betraying hint of satisfaction. He looked a little worn, after the responsibilities that had fallen on him in the last month, but he was invariably gravely polite, a man who weighed his words and betrayed very little emotion.

He inquired politely after the health of her family, but for once seemed a little less at ease than usual. He paced the room a little absently for a moment, then seemed at last to come to a decision. "Mademoiselle Reggie, I flatter myself that you and I are much alike," he said, coming to a halt before her. "We are both foreigners here, and that gives us a certain bond. I also believe we are alike in that we come from a broader, more sophisticated world. It cannot have escaped your notice that I have come to enjoy our—little chats together as almost the only bright spot in a somewhat difficult position. That is why . . . I have nerved myself to speak, even though it may be too soon. You may not realize it, my dear, but I am a very lonely man."

She guessed then what was coming, and her heart sank. She did what she could to try to prevent the coming declaration by saying quickly, in one of her rallying speeches, "What, with all the beauties in Burgos making up to you? That I will never believe."

He gave his somewhat weary smile. "It pleases you to be sportive. It is perhaps one of the things I most admire about you, my dear. My countrymen, you must know, admire wit more highly than most—especially in a beautiful woman."

She longed for an interruption—any interruption, but the Spanish servants were too well trained to interrupt when the French commandant was calling, and Conchita was not due back for another hour. She had, perforce, to listen to the measured flow of words.

"It is, however, but one of the things I admire in you," he went on warmly. "I have known you for some years, under trying circumstances, and I think I can safely say that you have never yet failed to excite my deepest admiration by your courage and charm. I will put it higher: even my strongest regard. That being the case, I would be more than honored if you would consent to become my wife."

She knew a pang at her double role, but even more horror at a situation that might well prove extremely dangerous to her. Nor could she help cursing herself for not having foreseen this, despite all Conchita's teasing. She said helplessly, "You flatter me, monsieur, far more than my due. But forgive me for pointing out that your wife has been dead but a few months."

He spread his thin hands. "I have made no attempt to hide the fact from you that the sad event did not leave me prostrate. My marriage was never a particularly happy one, and we had been apart for many years. I do you the honor of believing you would not wish me to pretend a heartache I do not feel."

"No, of course not. But you have caught me all unaware. I had no idea—"

"Ah, I feared I had perhaps been too precipitate," he conceded. "But there are good reasons why it seemed best to me not to wait any longer in proffering my suit. I will admit my own natural wishes are perhaps the strongest of those, for I have a very real desire to make up for lost time, so to speak."

"Monsieur, I don't know what to say," she said truthfully. "Except that I am deeply flattered and honored. I have a great respect and liking for you, but I never considered—especially since I believed you to be a married man. I, too, have enjoyed our little chats, but I must admit frankly that the possibility of a marriage between us never occurred to me. We have been thrown together, as you say, perhaps because we are both foreigners here. Is it possible you are mistaking that . . . for a—a—warmer regard? And even if not, you must know that my duty to my family is not such that I feel I can—entertain even so flattering a proposal at this time."

He looked surprised. "Is it so? I had naturally thought that when your stepsister married, you would be left at something of a loose end. It is partly that that dared me to proffer my suit at this time. It cannot be easy for you as a foreigner during these trying times."

"And there is that, too," she said daringly. "Have you forgotten I am English? I cannot think such a marriage would further your own career, monsieur. Have you thought of that?"

"I have naturally, of course. I do not think it will jeopardize my career, but it may do much to strengthen your own position, my dear Mademoiselle Reggie. I hesitated to mention it, for fear of seeming to unfairly press my suit, but you must know there has been some . . . talk lately. I have done what I can to scotch it, but I dare not completely disregard it."

Her heart was suddenly beating faster. "Talk—about me?" she demanded a little breathlessly.

"I regret so. I am sorry to say that your nationality has recently been remembered, in some quarters, and remarked upon. Where before your presence here was known, but by and large forgotten, now it has raised unworthy suspicions in a few minds. I thought you should know."

"And do you—believe these suspicions yourself?" she asked with a dry throat.

"I think, under the circumstances, you need not ask that," he answered her gravely. "I know you to be largely unpolitical, as, I confess, I am myself. It little matters to us what government we live under, or who rules us. I am a Frenchman, yes, but I go where I am sent, without troubling myself overmuch why or what is to happen, as do you, clearly. The very fact you have received me so graciously proves my point, I think."

She had to steel herself not to betray herself once more. "Th-thank you," she said inadequately. "But I cannot believe I am in any real danger."

"Let us hope not. I had hoped, I confess, that it would be

easier to protect you if I were known to be your fiancé—or even your husband. But I do not mean to hold that over your head, I assure you. You may count on me to do what I can to serve you, now and always."

By dint of falling back on her responsibilities to her family and the uncertain state of her stepfather's health, she was able to fob him off at last, if only for the moment. She dared not give him a direct refusal, much as she longed to, for both her own safety and the hope of further valuable information would seem to depend upon remaining on friendly terms with him.

But after he had gone at last, she sank onto a sofa, both uncertain and more than a little alarmed, knowing that whether or not he meant to hold it over her head, the threat had been there and was very real. She could only pray that if she continued to refuse him he would not one day use it against her.

Chapter 13

THE SECOND EVENT was even more unexpected. Reggie woke from a troubled sleep to sit bolt upright in bed, convinced there was someone else in the room. "Who's there?" she demanded abruptly, her eyes trying to penetrate the darker corners. Then, as the dregs of sleep departed and reason took hold, she added, less sharply, "Filipe? Is that you?"

There was a silence, then a voice she knew far too well said quietly from the darkness, "No, it's me. Adam."

"Adam!" It seemed, for one incredulous instant, that she must still be dreaming. Then she shook herself and fumbled to turn up the lantern left burning at her bedside, in case of just such nocturnal visits, annoyed that her hands were trembling and her heart was pounding so thunderingly in her chest she feared he must hear it from where he stood.

At last she had enough light to illuminate the room properly. For a moment she still could not see him; then he melted from the darkness and came toward the bed, saying lightly, "Accept my apologies. It's highly scandalous of me to be here, and even more unconscionable of me to wake you at such an hour, but I didn't know how else to do it, and I wanted to see you."

But she had temporarily forgotten all modesty in her rush to drink in the sight of him. Besides, she was too used to Filipe's unpredictable visits to be overly self-conscious. "No, no, don't be absurd! But are you all right? How did you get here? Why—what—?"

He was again, she saw, in his guise as a Spanish peasant, but he looked tired and drawn, and thinner than she remembered him. She added more sharply, knowing the answer already from that first glimpse of him, "Were you with the siege, then?"

He sighed. "Yes, for a while. And part of the retreat. But I've spent the last weeks in the north with the guerillas. That's how I came to make your stepbrother's acquaintance, who kindly made me a present of the existence of the secret door. I hope you don't mind my using it, but I couldn't leave the area without seeing you first and making sure you were all right. And I could hardly knock at the front door and inquire if you were at home to visitors."

"Filipe? You met Filipe?" she asked incredulously. But her mind was on other things and the question was almost automatic. Without hesitation she thrust back the bedclothes and climbed out of bed, slipping on her wrapper and ignoring her bare feet and her hair hanging untidily down her back, even as she ignored the somewhat embarrassing terms of their last meeting. All of that could wait. In fact, it no longer seemed to matter. "Never mind. Come down to the kitchens and I'll get you something to eat and drink. You look as if you could use it. Don't worry. The servants all sleep at the top of the house, and it won't matter if Conchita hears us."

He made a mild protest, which she wholly ignored, and then shrugged, objecting only to her bare feet and insisting she put on some slippers. "For I won't have it on my conscience knowing you caught pneumonia for my sake on top of everything else," he said with a ghost of his old grin. "And are you sure that flimsy robe you're wearing, fetching as it is, is warm enough? I would offer you my cloak, but it's somewhat the worse for wear, and none too clean, not to mention being quite wet. And I'm afraid I'm dripping all over your rug in a most unforgivable manner. It would seem I'm a most troublesome visitor, but then you should be used to that by now."

She saw then that he was indeed soaked, and bracing himself to keep from shivering with the cold. She said firmly, "There are some of Filipe's clothes in the next room. Come down when you've changed." And left him to it.

Somewhat to her surprise, he meekly did as she bid. For her part she hurried down to build up the kitchen fire again, and began carving bread and meat and cheese. There was some chicken left in the larder as well, in addition to some soup, which she set on the hob to heat, and some of the apple tart left from Don Ottavio's dinner. She ruthlessly took it all, reflecting ruefully as she set it out that poor Maria would come down to find her larder raided yet again in the morning.

He appeared quickly enough, attired in Filipe's clothes, which were slightly too small for him, and with his hair roughly dried. He spread his own cloak before the fire to dry and took a seat at the immense kitchen table. But when she set a full plate in front of him he merely looked at it for some moments, as if he had forgotten all about food. She suspected he took up his knife and fork merely to please her, for he was too weary to eat; and it was only as he began to spoon up the soup that he seemed to realize how hungry he was. Soon he was almost wolfing the food down.

She watched him quietly, taking in the changes in him since last she had seen him. From the signs, she knew without asking that the last few months had been very bad indeed, and felt almost ashamed of her own minor difficulties.

At last he finished and pushed aside his plate, saying ruefully, "Good Lord! I didn't realize I was so hungry. But I don't know when I last ate, if you want to know the truth, and that was marvelous. But I didn't come to have you looking after me, again. It seems I'm always turning up like the bad penny, in need of succor."

She poured him another glass of Don Ottavio's best claret, and at his insistence poured one for herself as well, though she only sat nursing it between her hands before the fire. There was a great deal to be said between them, and questions to be asked and answered, but for the moment she was merely content to have him there, while the rest of the house slept. It didn't matter why he had come or that he would undoubtedly soon be leaving again. All that mattered was that he was somehow miraculously there at that moment, still alive and safe.

Again he seemed to almost read her thoughts, for he sighed and said, "God, how peaceful this is! And how much I wish this were all there was to life. A quiet meal by the fire, with the war and its bloody demands a million miles away. I wish I need never leave again."

When she could at last control her voice, she asked steadily, "Was it very bad?"

"Bad?" He spoke with a lack of emphasis that was far more telling than anything else could have been. "Yes, it was bad. I hate all sieges! Backbreaking, murderous work, with no enemy to really come to grips with. I'd face a dozen pitched battles before I'd willingly undertake another. And the worst of it was we'd no hope of succeeding. The men knew it as well. It makes it—difficult to face them and try to put heart into them, to say the least."

"Then why did Wellington undertake it?" she inquired, troubled. "The French boasted that he had only brought a part of his forces, insufficient to the task."

He grimaced. "They were right, damn them. As to why he undertook it, I'm not in his confidence, I thank God. I'd not have his responsibilities for anything you could give me. The retreat was even worse, if possible, and I was only there for a part of it. As usual the commissariat had been sent on a different road from the troops, and the men were without supplies for days. That, after a month of siege work. When I left they were dropping like flies."

She took that in, trying not to picture the cheerful men she had seen, and wondering which of them were dead now, left for the carrion birds to pick clean. "Where did you go then?" she asked quietly after a while.

"To the north, to work with the guerillas. That's where I met Filipe." He summoned a brief smile, though it was obviously an effort. "Hotheaded, reckless young devil! I liked him. God knows I wish there were more like him in the country."

The question had to be asked, however much pain it caused. "And where do you go next?"

He shrugged. "Back to winter quarters, somewhere in Portugal. And from there, God knows. At the moment I'd like never to move again."

She had never seen him like this before. Tired and defeated and his energy at its lowest ebb, there was little of the charming, handsome major she had lost her heart to to be seen. And it seemed it didn't matter, for she thought her heart would burst in that moment with love and pity for him. There were certainly no moonbeams in evidence now, and he was too tired to remember the kisses they had shared or the things that had been said, some in anger, some in a very different emotion.

But none of that mattered. She was indeed more of a fool than she had yet guessed. Her only thought was that she was glad that his exhaustion had wiped out any possible constraint between them and that she was able to help him, if only by warm garments and a little food.

And perhaps he felt the same, for certainly he had never talked to her like this before. As if realizing it, he looked up and smiled tiredly. "But enough of that. What of you? You and your family made it through the siege safely? I thought of you often, believe me, and wished there was some way I could get word through to you."

"Oh, yes." It was clearly no time to burden him with her own troubles. "The guns were the worst of it. I doubt I would ever get used to the pounding. But we were never in any danger."

He grimaced. "Well, at least you should be safe enough

here now til spring. I—was wrong to try to send you away for my own convenience, I admit. I had some long talks with your stepbrother, while I was there, and he has convinced me of the worth of the work you are doing. He admires you very much, you know. And even if I can't like the risk you are taking, so do I. I have always said you were quite a girl, Reggie Alderstock."

She was at last embarrassed, where none of the unusual circumstances so far had driven her to self-consciousness. "Yes, I am a heroine, and Filipe is a hero, and we all know Major Adam Canfield is the most staid of soldiers!" she countered, annoyed to find herself blushing like a school-girl.

But he was scarcely listening. He was looking at her, across the table, in the firelight, as if he were seeing her that evening for the first time. As perhaps he was. Her cheeks grew hotter as she realized what she must look like, with her hair tumbled down her back and a loose wrapper over her nightdress, where before it had not mattered.

He continued to look at her steadily, for a long moment. Then unexpectedly he reached out a hand and touched her hot cheek lightly with one finger. "I shall remember you like this," he said deeply. "Not the cool, collected Miss Alderstock of my first acquaintance, nor yet the beautiful young lady at the ball, having her head turned by candle-light and compliments, however much I treasure those memories. But like this. My Reggie, disheveled and brave and still warm from her bed."

She could find nothing at all to say. The touch of his finger still burned on her skin, and she knew she had no defenses against him this time.

Then, abruptly, he withdrew his hand and thrust himself up with a muttered oath. "And God knows I had better go before it's too late," he said roughly. He went with a grimace to feel his damp cloak.

Reggie did not remember rising herself. But at least some vestige of sense and self-preservation made her latch on to that humdrum act. "Take one of Filipe's cloaks," she said rather hoarsely. "That one will never keep you warm." Then she blurted the one thing she vowed above all others not to say. "Must you go tonight? It is so wet and you are so tired."

He smiled, as if some of his charm and energy were seeping back into him with the fire and the hot soup. "Bless you, my dear, but I have known more wet hours in the saddle than dry ones. And I fear my business won't wait. It seems we are always fated to be saying goodbye to each other."

But his more normal voice had at least broken the spell. She hurried around, packing him up the sandwiches she had made ready, and several bottles of the claret and going to fetch one of Filipe's warm cloaks for him. She feared at any moment to break down, and so kept her head down, grateful for the small tasks. Fool! she berated herself. She had known from the moment he appeared that he would leave again. And the last thing he wanted in his present state were emotional leave-takings. "At least this will last you for a day or so."

He accepted the little bundle of food, still watching her, a twisted half smile on his lips. "Yes. Thank you. My dear—"

"Yes, you must go," she interrupted brightly, desperately fighting back the tears. "I fear I've kept you too long as it is, for it will soon be dawn."

"And e from every other consideration, it would scarcely do your reputation any good if I were to be found here," he said ruefully.

"That doesn't matter. But you—will—take care of yourself, won't you?"

"That from you?" he mocked her gently. He was in Filipe's cloak, now, and soon, far too soon, he would be gone again, for who knew how many months this time.

"Reggie." Abruptly he lifted her chin with his hand, to force her eyes up to him. For a moment it was so silent she could hear the fire shifting in the grate, and she feared her heart was there for him to read in her eyes, but she seemed powerless to do anything about it. "My dear—I am trying to be wise, but you make it damnably hard to leave you."

Then she was in his arms, and she was never to know who had made the first move. For a long time he held her almost desperately, so tightly that she feared her ribs would crack, her face buried in his neck and one hand unsteadily stroking her long, unloosed hair. Her heart was pounding so loudly she knew he must feel it, so closely were they bound, and she could feel his own heart beating as precipitately under her ear.

Then he had loosed her the space of a breath, and was kissing her, desperately, hungrily, and she could only wrap her arms tightly around his neck and cling to him, as feverishly as he. There was no room left for thoughts of right or wrong, or self-protection or fear of giving herself away, and for once he seemed to have lost his careful control as well.

Then at last—far too soon—he put her away from him almost forcibly, breathing hard as if he dared not trust himself any longer. The next moment he had snatched up his bundle of food and was gone.

She sat, dry-eyed, by the dying fire until a startled Maria found her there the next morning, and scolding and questioning her sharply, sent her up to bed.

But long afterward, even when she was most in danger, Reggie was at least glad to know that she had not broken down and burdened him with her own fears that night, on top of everything else. Monsieur de Thierry's proposal and the rising talk about her were weapons she would never willingly use against him, not if she died for them.

It was the one piece of her shattered pride she had left to her.

Chapter 14

Major Canfield strode into his quarters almost a week later, again tired and filthy, and created something of a sensation among his friends.

They were consuming a large and leisurely breakfast, and the small cottage they had commandeered as a billet was strewn with all the haphazard paraphernalia of young officers in the unaccustomed leisure of winter quarters. Military coats and shakos were thrown carelessly onto chairs to be donned again shortly, and whips and a hunting horn shared the happy confusion with a pair of wet boots placed before the fire to dry.

"Adam!" exclaimed Captain Prescott, his ugly face for once grinning broadly. "By all that's holy! We had almost given you up for dead this time!" He rose to eagerly shake his hand.

The other two men in the room had also risen and now clamored around, shaking the newcomer's hand or buffeting him playfully on the shoulder. "Good God! It's about time you got here. The place has been dead without you," exclaimed Captain Colville.

Adam fended off their exuberant greetings and dropped wearily into a chair before the fire. "No, no. You should know by now I bear a charmed life. But not as charmed as you, I see. How in the devil did you manage to commandeer such a snug cottage? I was sure I would find you in a mud hut, as we were last year."

"Oh, you must credit young Austerby here for that," said

Colville. "He had the presence of mind to make up to the owner's daughter, who gladly turned it over to us, preferring to trust us rather than some of those careless fellows in other divisions!"

Adam looked around at the confusion in the room. "Poor deluded fellow. God, it's good to be back," he said tiredly. "Is there any of that food left, or have you vandals eaten it all? I can't remember when I last had a meal."

Captain Prescott had already calmly gone to set another plate for him, while Colville teased, "At least some things never change. We might have known you'd turn up half starved, as usual. Not to mention looking like something the cat dragged in. My dear fellow, where *did* you get that coat?"

The major did indeed look odd in those surroundings, for he was still in his peasant garb, and a week's hard riding had not improved them any. He grinned, but it seemed only a perfunctory gesture. "Lord yes," he agreed, digging hungrily into the food. "I've almost forgotten what a bath is, while you lazy fellows sit around in the lap of luxury. Only tell me, why Frenada? I had the devil of a job finding you, and I confess it would not have been my first choice for winter quarters."

"How you intelligence men do it!" marveled Captain Colville in amusement. "In fact the place is cold, bleak, and damnably windy, not to mention being full of fleas and without one redeeming feature that we've been able to discover. But we've only been here a month now, whereas you discovered the place's disadvantages immediately."

"Oh, I daresay there's method in Old Hookey's madness, as usual," corrected Captain Prescott in his calm way, taking his place again at the table. "In fact I strongly suspect he chose it for no other reason than its distance from Lisbon, where the Portuguese regency and any number of distinguished English visitors are even now ensconced. You must know, my dear Adam, that he has become a great man since last you saw him. A marquisate, no less, awarded by a grateful British Parliament. His lordship is said to have re-marked in his irascible way, when he received the news, 'What the devil is the use of making me a marquess? Why don't they send me some cannon instead?'"

Adam grinned again, still addressing himself hungrily to his meal. "Well, I'm all for it if it will get them to increase our supplies any," he agreed. "By the by, where the devil did you manage to come by bacon? Am I dreaming, or has the commissariat at last caught up with us?"

"You're dreaming. My dear boy, the one thing we can count on in this uncertain world is that the commissariat will have been sent on a different road from the troops whenever we are the most hardpressed," remarked Captain Colville. "In my opinion Gordon should be hung—and he came nearer to it than he knew on that last retreat, if the men had had anything to do with it. But you don't seriously think this bacon came from the commissariat, do you? We've seen nothing but moldy flour and weevily beef! And glad enough to get that on occasion, I can tell you."

"In fact," put in Lord George irrepressibly, "this was a gift from our host. I told you my *beaux yeux* would come in useful some day. You none of you appreciate me properly."

"That at least is true. But your *beaux yeux* had nothing to do with it, my poor deluded young fool," retorted the impi-ous Colville. "He may as well have presented us with it, for he'd no hope of preserving it from this horde. Especially after the last few months."

Adam looked up, his mouth rather overfull of bacon. "Yes, tell me about that," he said quietly. "I had to leave, but the retreat seemed an ill-managed enough affair."

"Ill-managed? I like your understatement. My dear fel-low, even old Hooknose afterward admitted it was the worst scrape we ever were in. But then speaking only for myself, of course, I like being chased by a hundred thou-sand French soldiers. Adds a certain zest to what would otherwise be an ignominious retreat. And really, consider-ing the odds, and the lack of rations, we lost surprisingly few men—only an odd six thousand or so, and most of them fell from starvation and exhaustion, not enemy action."

Captain Prescott was looking grave. "Yes," he agreed quietly, "it was a near-run thing. And if the troops hadn't been who they are, we would indeed have met with disaster that time."

"My dear Prescott, what can you be thinking of?" corrected Colville in mock astonishment. "That scum of the earth? You must know, Adam, that as usual Gordon had sent the supply wagons along a different route from the troops. For four days the men received no rations. And that after a month of siege duty. They were dropping from the ranks like flies. It's little wonder the ingenious bastards robbed cottages on the way, shot up herds of pigs, and stole beehives. But did the great and newly minted Marquis of Wellington show any appreciation for the narrow squeak we had gotten him out of? He did not! Instead we have had a thundering letter which has somehow been leaked to the men, and they are all rightly furious."

"I doubt he knew the supply wagons had gone astray," pointed out Captain Prescott in his calm way.

"No, for if he did he might perhaps do something about it! But that is not all he was gracious enough to be displeased about. Oh, no. He had a list of grievances as long as my arm, going back to the withdrawal from Madrid in September. By the by, that was another enjoyable experience you missed out on, my dear Adam. The Spanish clung to us in the streets, begging us not to leave. It was damned embarrassing, I can tell you. And then, when they saw there was no help for it, the same ones who had been calling us their saviors turned on us and could scarcely be contained in their fury. Ah, what it is to be a soldier."

"Aye, but his lordship's had much to vex him of late," put in the ever-reasonable Captain Prescott. "But enough of this. What have you been up to all this time, Adam?

Robert's right. We had begun to fear you dead or captured."

Adam gave a jaw-cracking yawn, then apologized for it. "Sorry, I can't seem to keep myself awake. I've been with the guerillas in the north, finding out what they know and doing what I can to organize them."

"Did you meet Miss Alderstock's brother while you were there?" inquired Prescott interestedly. "He is with the guerillas in the north, as I recall."

"I did. And then I dropped in on Burgos to see Miss Alderstock herself."

His calm announcement created something of a new sensation. "And I suppose you left your visiting card at the French general's house?" retorted young Lord George, taking it as a joke. "What a complete hand you are, Adam!"

The two others knew him rather better. After a pause, Captain Prescott said calmly, "I trust she is well? The late siege must have been as uncomfortable for her as it was for us."

"Yes, she is well," retorted Adam shortly. "Unfortunately, she's taken it into her head to serve as liaison between her brother and the other guerilla groups."

"Taken it into her head—upon my soul!" ejaculated Colville unwisely. "I know she delivered that one message for you, and I have no doubt she's a damn brave girl, but are you sure that's wise? I mean——" He then broke off, realizing he was being tactless, as Prescott kicked him hastily under the table.

"I daresay she's in little enough danger," commented Captain Prescott in his calm way. "As I recall, her Spanish relations are very well respected, and she's a particular friend of the French commandant there. I don't say it's ideal, but there's no denying she's a most redoubtable girl. A woman of uncommon spirit and courage, in fact."

"She is that. And a damned little fool!" Abruptly Adam pushed aside his empty plate and rose. "Lord, I must change clothes and then report in. Don't eat all the food before I get back."

"Good God, get some sleep first, man!" urged Captain Colville with rough concern, his ankle forgotten. "You're dead on your feet."

Adam yawned again. "If I do, I fear I'll sleep for a week. I can't remember when was the last time I saw a bed. God, I'm beginning to loathe this war!"

After he had gone, the two older officers exchanged glances again, both of them frowning this time. It was Lord George who said in puzzlement, "He *must* be tired, poor fellow. He didn't seem at all himself, did you notice?"

After a moment Captain Prescott said dryly, "He's worried, I expect."

"Worried? What has he to be worried about? Oh, you mean Miss Alderstock? But she's safe enough, as Prescott said, surely?"

Neither one of them answered him. It was Colville who said with violence, "The devil! It's a good thing you kicked me. Do you think that affair can be serious? He certainly appears to be taking it badly, and I've never known him do that before."

"Your guess is as good as mine. But something is bothering him."

"Affair?" repeated Lord George in sudden enlightenment. "What, you don't mean Miss Alderstock? Well I'll be! If so, it's a good thing, if you ask me. Devilish fine girl! Just the sort of spirited girl to suit old Adam."

"If she lives to suit old Adam," remarked Colville dryly. "Passing on military secrets to the guerillas sounds like a dangerous pastime for any woman, I would have said, but especially for an Englishwoman behind enemy lines."

"Then why doesn't Adam marry the girl and whisk her away to safety?" demanded Lord George, exasperated. "Exactly the sort of thing in his line—a dramatic rescue and all that. Never knew such a fellow for positively enjoying sticking his head into danger."

There was another silence. It was again Colville who explained, "Then it's obvious you haven't heard his diatribe against women in the tail of the army, my poor innocent. Leading a hellish life and creating divided loyalties for the officer, and all that. One of the few things I've ever seen him get really worked up over, as a matter of fact."

"Oh, I don't know," said Lord George. "Seems tempting, sometimes. After a tiring day in battle, come home to find a hot supper waiting and a loving wife to comfort you, don't you know. Doesn't sound at all bad."

"And who is to protect the loving wife while you're engaged in that tiring battle? No, Adam's right. It's never seemed a life for a woman to me," agreed Captain Colville.

"Unless, of course, she is setting herself up to pass on military secrets," remarked Captain Prescott wryly. "And I suspect Adam is learning that he has all of the worries and none of the advantages in his present situation. Poor devil. I don't envy him a bit."

It seemed to be Reggie's time for late-night visitors. She woke only a week after Adam's unexpected visit to find her stepbrother Filipe sitting on the edge of her bed, smelling of the rain and outdoors, and as cheerful as ever.

It was all she could do not to throw her arms around him. He had not dared try to penetrate into the city during the month-long siege, so that it seemed an age since she had last seen him. "Oh, Filipe! Thank God!"

"*Dios* had nothing to do with it," he grinned. "The stupid French guards are full of brandy tonight to ward off a chill."

He was, as usual, ravenously hungry, and while the devoted Maria fed him, in her nightgown and an enormous wrapper, her graying hair down her back in a long braid, he regaled Reggie and his sister with the tale of his exploits since they had last seen him.

"Oh, we have been having an amusing time of it," he grinned, biting into a cold leg of chicken. "The English re-

treat gave us some useful opportunities. We managed to
capture one lagging company of French grenadiers, guns
and supplies and all—not to mention five hundred dollars!
More, they had decent clothes, which we were sorely lacking. We made them switch with us on the spot—you notice
my new and excellent boots, I hope!—and sent them back
under parole. Their captain was so humiliated I really
feared he might shoot himself on the spot."

"But why did you let them go?" demanded Conchita,
likewise in her wrapper and, as always, clutching one of her
brother's hands as if she could not bear to let go of him.

"That is the greatest laugh of all!" managed Filipe, between sips of strong coffee. "We couldn't keep them prisoners because they outnumbered us by a considerable
margin. That is what made it so particularly humiliating for
them. That and having to give up their boots, and often
even their breeches, and taking our ragged ones in return. I
have never seen a more dejected troop march away. We
could not help laughing."

"Yes, but that reminds me that I have managed to obtain
some new clothes for you," put in Conchita contentedly,
rubbing her cheek against his hand.

"*Muchas gracias!* I need them. And how is your es-
teemed *novio*? Which reminds me, Reggie, I met your English officer. He came to coordinate with us—at least that is
the polite term he used. But I don't doubt his orders were to
organize the 'squabbling and frequently far too independent
guerilla bands'—I am quoting from one of the more polite
things it is reputed the British commander calls us!—into a
dependable asset. He did, too, within an inch of our lives.
And the funny thing is, he did it with such skill not even
Sanchez was offended, or guessed that we had been oh-so
delicately converted into serving as mere support for the
British army."

"Yes, yes, we know all about that," put in Conchita irrepressibly. "Major Canfield was here before you. It was
most exciting! I am only sorry I missed seeing him."

Filipe transferred his bright gaze to Reggie. "Well, well, what is this? Don't tell me a romantic tryst?"

"What, at my age?" demanded Reggie mournfully, refusing to blush.

Filipe laughed. "Ah! He is a good man. I liked him. But he was much concerned about you, little *Inglesa*. He wished me to try to use my influence with you to send you back to England."

"And did you promise?"

"I told him the truth, that I had no influence. Since the day you moved in, a gawky fourteen-year-old, you have ruled us all with an iron rod."

"Be kind!" insisted Conchita hotly. "I do not know where we would all be without dearest Reggie. But I fear it is true that she would be safer in England. You do not know it, *mi Filipe*, but Monsieur de Thierry has warned her there are starting to be rumors about her in the town. Especially when the English were besieging us it was remembered that she is, after all, English herself. I confess it frightens me. I know the English failed last time, but I very much fear they will try again."

"You may well fear it," agreed Filipe more soberly. "Wellington knows Burgos is the key to all French communications. He can't afford not to take it. But you are saying the governor himself warned Reggie? Well, well again."

"Oh, you do not know that either! I am forgetting it has been so long since we've seen you. He proposed marriage to her. *Por Dios* I would have laughed, for I have been telling her forever that he is in love with her and she would not believe me, except that I am so very worried. It will be most awkward if she is obliged to refuse him, for I hear he will withdraw his support, and then she *will* be in danger."

Filipe whistled. "You have been busy, my English sister. But perhaps you had better accept his offer. If the French should succeed in beating the British, which most sane advisors would tell you they will, it might prove most useful to be so closely related to the French commandant."

"But then the French are not going to defeat the British," Reggie said calmly.

"I wish I might believe it. But after that last foolish siege—No, Filipe, despite my teasing it is no laughing matter," insisted Conchita. "I have been trying to tell her it would be safest if she returned to Madrid. Filipe, *you* tell her so. *El Mejor* Canfield is right. Maria and I can carry on here without her, and we are in much less danger than she is. We can safely pass on whatever messages are necessary."

"On the contrary, you are in a good deal more," Reggie retorted. "Alone, I shudder to think what difficulties you might not get into. Besides, you have your father to think of."

"She has you there, 'Chita!" agreed Filipe mischievously. "Between the pair of you it would be hard to choose which is the more guileless. You would betray yourselves immediately."

"So that settles it. At any rate, I assure you I am in no real danger," Reggie said firmly.

"Which reminds me that I have a message for you to pass on through the usual channels," confessed Filipe. "It concerns supplies for the coming assault in the spring."

"Then there will be another assault?" asked Reggie quickly.

"Oh, of a certainty. Wellington may have failed in his first assault, but you may be sure he will try again. They don't know it yet, but the French are on the way out. And if it galls me to owe the restoration of my country to the English, I will take the eviction of the cursed French any way I can get it."

He finished off a huge wedge of cheese, and sighed. "But Conchita is right to be concerned. Shall I get you out and to Madrid, Reggie? It is, after all, my country's fight, and not yours."

"What is it in men that makes them consider patriotism and loyalty a purely masculine trait?" demanded Reggie with some asperity. "First Major Canfield, and now you. Would you so lightly turn your back on your duty in the face of a little danger? You risk your life every day of the week and think nothing of it, because you believe in what you are doing. Well, so do I. And more than you, I have two countries to fight for, not merely one."

"Peace! Peace!" cried Filipe, holding up his hand in a fencer's gesture. "I cry pardon. Anyway," he grinned, "I told Adam you would not leave. But I am charged to get word to him if you are ever in danger. Then, my dear sister, he will get you out by hook or by crook, whatever your loyalties or wishes. I suspect you will have very little choice in the matter. He struck me as a most determined man, your British major."

Chapter 15

Spring, Summer, 1813

FILIPE HAD BEEN away before dawn, again loaded with supplies and Conchita's precious new clothes, which he had donned on the spot. He also left several messages for Reggie to pass on, and had slipped out with a cheery wave and a grin.

It was more than obvious that he, like Adam, felt no hesitation about heading back to certain danger and likely death. For the first time it occurred to Reggie to wonder what he would find to do if the war indeed ever ended. Would he be content to go back to university, or had the lure of danger and excitement spoiled him forever for the ordered life he would ordinarily have lived, as heir to his father and a respected Spanish citizen?

It was a sobering thought that kept recurring to her during the spring months of that new year. What would they all do, if and when the war was finally over? Everyone, like herself, whose life had been changed forever by the course of the war. Filipe and his fellow guerillas were young men of good family who might find their taste for the old life they had risked their lives to protect was no longer there. And Adam and all the British soldiers, who had spent so many years in a foreign climate, would find it strange and foreign to return to the country they had been fighting for. Or herself, who no longer knew who she might have been if the war had not intervened. Would she have been back in

England even now, safely married and the mother of a numerous brood?

It was a difficult question to answer, particularly since as the spring progressed it grew harder and harder to believe the war would ever be over, let alone the French defeated. The British advance was late that year, and rumors continued to circulate in the town that Wellington had learned his lesson and the British troops had lost heart after their failure to take Burgos.

The *Moniteur,* the official French newspaper that Reggie read, with much contempt, for information, said openly that Wellington had tacitly conceded defeat. Even his own Parliament did not support him, and he would undoubtedly be recalled soon. In the meantime, the English commander-in-chief was reported to be too taken up with foxhunting and frivolity in his winter cantonments to have time for planning campaigns. He and his effete young officers had even given a ball in Rodrigo, in a building in which there had been a shell hole in the roof and another in the dance floor, the one hidden by stolen tapestries, and the other with a sentry stationed to warn the dancers. It was little wonder the stern French soldiers of the motherland would so easily defeat them for good this summer.

Reading this, Reggie merely found herself wishing with all her heart that she could have been at the ball. She could easily picture them there, all her new friends, dancing and cracking jokes and ignoring the holes in the floor or the shabby nature of their own uniforms. Burgos, that had so long been her home, seemed the alien place with its French soldiers.

Whether talk had indeed begun to arise about her, as Monsieur de Thierry had suggested, as March passed and then April, and no new crisis arose, she gradually began to relax. Some of the French in town were admittedly cool to her, but no one said anything directly to her, and so long as Monsieur de Thierry continued to visit her, she thought she was relatively safe.

The latter had not yet given any indication of using her precarious position as a polite club against her, as she had half feared he might. In fact, he behaved toward her with impeccable Gallic courtesy, so that she came even to feel slightly guilty about her suspicions. He did continue, however, to assume, where she was concerned, a slight proprietary air that set her teeth on edge, but which she dared not object to, and he kept her supplied with more hard-to-obtain food and luxury items, which she unashamedly made use of to pass on to Filipe. She also unashamedly used the preparations for Conchita's now fast-approaching wedding as an excuse for not giving him an answer, and wondered somewhat desperately what would happen when that would no longer work.

Then, in late May word came at last that the English were on the move, and Filipe reappeared with a young fugitive he wished her to hide.

The first began unprosperously enough, according to report, for the late spring rains hampered the army's movements. It was not until May 22 that the English army marched, and only gradually did it become clear that Wellington had succeeded in pulling off a major coup. The French marshals had gotten into the habit of believing the marquis always moved with his main body, and thus ignored the advance toward the north of a larger body under Graham to concentrate on Wellington's movements.

In four days this smaller troop under Wellington had regained Salamanca and were moving on Toro. And it was only then that Wellington's trick became obvious. With a few staff officers he galloped furiously from Salamanca at dawn on May 29, and crossed the Douro next morning in a basket hauled by cable. By noon he had joined Graham's main body, and on June 3 made junction with Hill at Toro. Within twelve days of starting he had managed to get eighty thousand men within striking distance of Valladolid.

Panic was renewed in Burgos, not helped by the fact that King Joseph and Marshal Jourdan, who hoped to intercept the British at Salamanca, were worried, and sent a huge convoy of refugees and plunder from Valladolid toward Burgos. It arrived in confusion and alarm, and suddenly the town was filled to bursting point with French military wives and mistresses, in their own elegant carriages or calèches, demanding places to stay. The huge convoy necessary to escort such a valuable train merely added to the confusion, not to mention herds of goats, sheep, mules and horses, asses and milch cows. It was rumored King Joseph's own possessions, including Italian pictures cut from their frames and looted from Madrid, and coins worth almost a million pounds sterling was also among the heavily guarded wagons.

Reggie was too preoccupied at the moment to pay much attention, and again could only be grateful for her friendship with the commandant that kept any of the French refugees from being quartered in their house. Elsewhere, any number of Spanish families of wealth and dignity had to endure the presence of the upstart French thrust upon them, or were even forced to give up their homes to them completely. Monsieur de Thierry used the excuse of Don Ottavio's illness to spare them that, and in light of her inconvenient guest, Reggie could only accept this further favor with relief, however much it might increase her debt to the commandant.

That it was placing her in an increasingly awkward position she had no time to worry about, for her fugitive, a young man from Vittoria, was presently wanted by the French for spying activities, and was both badly frightened and in ill health. He had spent nearly a week in hiding in the pouring rain, and was shaking with the ague when Filipe brought him.

He stammered out his thanks through chattering teeth, and was glad enough to go to bed and leave his fate to her and Filipe. Filipe was also tired and wet, but he could not stay. He grabbed a hurried meal as he apologized for bringing her such a live coal at such a time. "But there was nothing else to do with him. The French will hang him if they find him, and the devil of it is none of us can spare the time to escort him ourselves. Well, you wanted to be part of the war, my English sister. With luck he will be well enough to leave for Madrid in a few days, but don't keep him longer than that in any case, for you are in too much danger as it is. And I fear that will only get worse, not better in the next few weeks."

She was surprised. "Why in the next few weeks?" Then she looked at him more closely. She only became aware then that despite his exhaustion there was a nervous tension about him that only then revealed itself as excitement.

He grinned, verifying the correctness of her guess, for his eyes shone and she had never quite seen him this keyed up. "The British are on the march and there will soon be the grandfather of all battles, unless I miss my guess. This is it!" he exulted. "The French will be rompéd at last, and besides the fact that every man will be needed, none of us would miss it for the world."

She did not know whether to be glad or apprehensive, but said automatically, "No, no, you did right to bring him. But he is very ill. I won't send him away before he is well enough to travel."

"Don't risk your own neck," said Filipe sharply. "I was teasing you earlier, for I promise if I'd had any other solution, I would never have brought him to you at such a time. In fact, it's not too late. Shall I send him on his way? I've no intention of trading your life to save his, and the chances are he would make it safely."

"Not in his present state, poor boy. No, I am safe enough," she assured him. "To tell truth, there is so much confusion in the town at the moment, I think I have been largely forgotten. I will have to get Father Gregorio to look at him, and we will hope that his care and a few days' rest will see the poor boy ready to travel. But don't worry about any of us. We go on well enough. And I have Monsieur de Thierry to protect me, don't forget."

He grinned again at that, but had to be satisfied, for he could not risk staying any longer. She knew as well as he did that he risked his life every time he slipped into the town, and that his safety was far more endangered by the current panic than she was.

But far from getting better, her patient grew steadily worse, and there could be no thought of moving him in a few days. Father Gregorio, her old friend, shook his head and looked grave, and indeed the news did nothing to make harboring a fugitive at such a time any safer.

For Wellington, after that first successful trick, was for once striking fear into the hearts of the heretofore insouciant French. Even those in Burgos conceded nervously that the British advance seemed unstoppable. The town, overcrowded and full of French refugees as it was, reacted hourly to a new panic, and emotions were running high between the French and their reluctant Spanish hosts. It was a volatile enough situation without the added complication of her own presence as an Englishwoman within the occupied town. And she could not but be aware of the further risk she ran sheltering the young fugitive at such a time.

There seemed no help for it, however, and she was more than once in the next few weeks to remember ruefully her boast that she was tired of leaving all the excitement to the male sex.

Nor were her misgivings misplaced. She soon found herself the object of stares and suspicion when she showed herself on the streets, and once or twice an ugly episode was only narrowly averted. Conchita, torn by her rapidly approaching marriage between a quiet joy there could be no denying, and guilt, begged her to give up her foolish independence and remain indoors, or else wear a veil as any respectable Spanish woman did when walking abroad.

But not only would Reggie's pride not allow her to give in so cravenly to such intimidation, but she suspected it would only add to the present tensions. Were she to betray any guilt or fear, things would only get worse, so that her only chance seemed to lie in brazening it through.

But it made for some tense times, and it was scarcely the safest moment to be harboring a young Spanish patriot wanted by the French.

Even so, she was unprepared for the day a grave Monsieur de Thierry was shown up to her. He looked unlike his usual reserved self, and came to the point almost straight away, which was also unlike him. "Mademoiselle—Reggie!—you must forgive me for bursting in upon you in the midst of your festivities. Your stepsister's wedding was to take place this week, I believe?"

"Yes, they were married yesterday," Reggie answered quietly, trying hard to subdue a sense of rising dread at his appearance. "They are even now on the bridal trip to Madrid."

"Ah. Accept my felicitations. The ceremony, under the circumstances, was naturally private. It is understood. Nor is it—quite the moment for—celebrations, I agree."

She pricked up her ears immediately. "Why is that? Have you heard something?"

"As to the war, nothing but what all the town has heard. Naturally I do not expect the town to fall, but I will not attempt to disguise from you that we have suffered some reverses. But that is not what I came to speak of. You did not consider accompanying your stepsister to Madrid, as you did once before? I am naturally loath to lose you, but it seems—a pity, under the circumstances."

Her premonition had been correct. She stiffened but said dryly, "On her honeymoon? Hardly. Besides, there is my stepfather to consider." Conchita had, in fact, tearfully begged her to accompany them, fearing for Reggie's safety in the war-torn town. But there was Don Ottavio to be considered, and the poor young fugitive, and Conchita had at last been reluctantly made to see how impossible the idea was.

Reggie added slowly now, dreading the answer, "What circumstances do you speak of?"

He took an uncomfortable turn about the room, then turned to face her reluctantly. "You will recall that I once warned you there were certain rumors about you in the town. They are naturally ridiculous. I need not reassure you, I hope, that I place not the slightest credence in them. But when a mob is frightened—?" he shrugged eloquently. "What have you? I promise you it has not been my wish to—press you upon that certain matter we spoke of once before. But I do not scruple to tell you that your position in this town now is—not a happy one. In short, I very much fear there remains only one way that I can continue to protect you as I desire."

When he hesitated again, she said, through frozen lips, "What are you saying?"

Again he appeared unwilling to put it into words. "That I very much fear I can no longer guarantee your safety unless you are my wife. I hope it is not necessary to add that it remains the dearest wish of my life to continue to serve and protect you and that you would be doing me an immense honor in consenting to wed me."

She was aware of a cold shaft thrusting down deep inside her, and recognized that the dilemma she had so long feared was at last upon her. Without the commandant's patronage she was in very real danger, and she knew it. She tried to close her mind to the report of the atrocities carried on by these same people during their revolution, but she had seen enough already of hatred and heightened emotions to know that the town could turn on her in an instant.

Thank God that Conchita was at least safely away. But there was still the frail and bedridden Don Ottavio to be considered, not to mention the rest of the household and her young fugitive, still too weak to think of traveling. Mobs fed on violence, and once begun could seldom be turned aside by claims of reason or compassion. She might be willing to risk her own life, but had she the right to risk the others as well?

And yet the alternative equally stopped her heart. Marriage to the French commandant seemed a small enough price to pay to protect herself and her family, but she was not at all sure she could make herself pay it. Even as she recognized with scorn the reason for that hesitation, she could not counter the dread rising up in her, or the horror.

Well, the moonbeams had long since disappeared in the cold reality of the day-to-day survival, and if memories of those few fevered moments by the firelight insisted upon intruding, she was undoubtedly a fool to balk at a marriage which might save her own and others' lives. Major Adam Canfield—but it did no good to think of him. He was busy with his own life, if he was still alive at all, and she was a romantic little fool indeed to dream of being rescued from what were no more than the fruits of her own sowing.

No, she had wanted to be freed from the woman's usual role of passive waiting. Well, she had now had her taste of dabbling in more dangerous waters, and if she found them no longer much to her liking, she should be prepared to make whatever sacrifice necessary to achieve her ends. A soldier risked his life every day. Why then did she hesitate to risk so much smaller a part of herself?

And yet she did hesitate, for reasons that had nothing to do with Adam. She had long accepted realistically that there was very little future for her there, no matter her secret longings. He had no use for a military wife, and she, despite everything, no desire to be settled in safety in England and promptly forgotten. Very well. She had come to terms with that. But marriage to anyone else, feeling as she did, was a very different matter.

She told herself firmly she was overly squeamish. She would certainly not be the first woman forced into a loveless marriage, and one that made her skin faintly crawl. She did not even despise Monsieur de Thierry. He was an honorable man who had been more than generous to her, and was perhaps risking his own reputation even now by offering to protect her with his name.

And yet the thought of marriage to him—the woman's traditional sacrifice, after all—made her feel weak and shaken, as if she were coming down with her patient's ague. The future—every day and every night—tied to this polite, rather gray man before her, who was also her enemy, seemed more than she could bear.

But did she have the right to make such finicking determinations when the lives of others might well hang in the balance? She had wanted her adventure. If it should have turned out to be more than she bargained for, she had no one to blame but herself.

The arguments could go on and on, but there was no time. He was standing there, polite and faintly embarrassed, waiting for an answer. She looked at him again, kind, earnest, a decent man, and heard herself saying, as if it were someone else's voice speaking and not her own, "You have been more than kind, *monsieur*. I would be—honored to become your wife."

Chapter 16

THE NEXT FEW days passed somehow, in a fog. Thankfully Monsieur de Thierry had been too taken up with more pressing matters to prove overly amorous. He had kissed her hand, and then her lips, and if it was all she could do not to flinch at even so mild an embrace, she told herself coldly that she had best learn to school her features better in future, when she was his wife.

His wife. The words struck a pang deep in her heart, and yet it was indeed a small enough price to pay. Filipe and Adam and the others risked their lives daily. Why then should she cavil at so much smaller a sacrifice for what she believed in?

It was by dint of such stern lectures to herself that she got though the days before her hurried wedding. She longed for Conchita, but that was foolish. She must be glad that Conchita was safely in Madrid for the moment. And to know Don Ottavio safe, and Maria and the others, not to mention her young fugitive, now mercifully recovering and soon strong enough to travel, must easily outweigh her own private hell. Besides, if the British assault was to fail a second time, she might still be needed there, to help Filipe and do what she could. As the commandant's wife, she would be in an even better situation to pass on valuable information, and perhaps put an end to the killing at last. That, too, made her own fears and bitter unhappiness seem petty by comparison.

Monsieur de Thierry, in light of the charged atmosphere

in the town, had placed armed guards in front of her house, and if that made her effectively a prisoner and was unpleasantly symbolic of the state she was about to enter, she had reason more than once to be grateful for the French soldiers' presence.

There had been several ugly incidents, confirming her in her reluctant belief that marriage to Monsieur de Thierry was her only solution. Once a mob gathered, shouting hateful and obscene threats at her, before they were at last driven away by the soldiers. And several times ugly epithets were scrawled on the walls of the house.

Reggie tried to at least keep the true state of affairs from her stepfather. But she should have known he was still too shrewd, even in his present frailty, to be fooled by her determinedly cheerful demeanor.

He stopped her once, as she was chatting of unimportant matters, to say weakly, "Do you believe me blind as well as in ill health, my daughter?"

She was taken so much by surprise that she was thrown, for a brief moment. "What—no, of course not, my dear sir! What on earth are you talking about?"

"I am talking about your determined cheerfulness when you come to see me, and the way you chatter of nothing, in the hopes of distracting me from the truth. Luckily, my old friend Gregorio is more truthful—or perhaps I should say, less of an actor."

He paused then, for he was so frail in those days that even talking could exhaust him. As if frustrated by his own weakness, he said under his breath, "*Dios!* If only I—But talking pays no toll. I am at the end of my days, and they have been full and happy ones, for the most part. It is only the scourge that falls upon my country now that makes me regret—but that, too, does no good to speak of. But I fear I have not done well by you, *mi hija*. I should have insisted you return to your own country on the death of your dear mother."

Reggie was having to fight back tears, for he never

talked like this to her, or betrayed his frustration with his illness. In his day he had been a man of power and strength, much as Filipe bid fair to becoming, and she had never doubted that his inability to help his country in need ate at him like a canker.

She took his hand rather tightly. "Dearest sir, you could not have been kinder to me if I had indeed been your daughter. And I hope you know that you have, in turn, become like a father to me."

He returned the clasp of her hand weakly. "Then if so, let us have no lies between us. Are you in danger?"

She could only pick her way carefully, fearful of upsetting him, but having no way of knowing how much the priest had seen fit to tell him. "Why, I don't think so. There have been a few unpleasant episodes, but I do not regard them." She decided the safest way was to appeal to his fierce love for his country, and added with a twinkle, "And in truth, I don't blame them either. For once Wellington has them terrified, and the French in the town are running around in a panic, one moment boasting that the British will never defeat them, and the next trying if they can to obtain some means of transport to rescue their belongings just in case he does!"

He smiled perfunctorily. "They are fools! I have always said so. In my day we would have sent them about their business years ago, Napoleon or no Napoleon. But I am not to be distracted. Gregorio tells me some nonsense that you are to wed the French commandant. Is that true?"

She felt, oddly, almost ashamed in that moment, but she had known she must tell him sooner or later. She said as lightly as she could, "Why, yes. You know him, and even admitted you respected him, if you could never like him. And I must marry someone. You know yourself that no respectable Spanish gentleman would willingly take such a firebrand as myself into his home. Monsieur de Thierry has been more than kind and even risked his own reputation to protect me."

He beat his weak fists in impotent rage against his blankets. "Do not try to hoodwink me, *hija*! What hold has he over you? Is it me? Do you sacrifice yourself to protect me?"

"Why no," she said coolly. "Indeed, he has no hold over me."

But he would not be convinced. "*Por Dios*, I am too old and weak and sick to protect my own, even!" he fretted. "I will not have you do this, child, do you hear me? Whatever your reasons, you are not to marry yourself to any dog of a Frenchman. I am not worth it!"

He was working himself up into one of his attacks, and she quietly gestured to his valet, a devoted man who had been with him for more than thirty years. "I beg you not to make yourself ill, dear sir. And I do not do it for you. I do it for myself. I could not live with myself if I chose my own happiness over that of so many others, any more than Filipe could, or you could have in your prime."

He had, perforce, to swallow some of the *tisana* that his valet was holding for him, and it seemed to help him somewhat, though he lay weak and spent on his pillows. "Ah," he managed in hoarse triumph. "So you do make a sacrifice in wedding this French dog. But, my child, if my country must demand such sacrifices of its women, then even I do not wish to see its independence again. And what of this British major you had hidden in the house and told me nothing about?"

She was shocked that he knew of him, and even the mention of him gave her a little jolt. But she managed to say serenely, "I hope he may be alive and well somewhere, but he does not come into it. And you do me less than justice, my dear sir. I love Spain almost as much as I love my own country, and I would not be worthy of you, or my own father, if I shrank from helping either in their hours of need. Now go to sleep. You have overexhausted yourself with these useless emotions, for when did you ever know me to be deflected from my chosen path, argue or threaten how you will?"

He was, indeed, almost asleep, but he chuckled tiredly at that. "*Sí*, you always were a handful. So unlike your gentle mother. I loved her, you know. I'm sorry she did not live to see you now . . . " His voice trailed off and he slept.

Reggie sat on beside his bed for a moment longer, grieving for the Titan she had once known, and for her mother, whom he had pampered and cherished as if she had been some precious hothouse flower.

It was an existence she herself would have soon smothered in, however, and it was a lesson she needed to remember now. Better her own difficult road than to be coddled and placed quite firmly out of the action, to do no more than wait to hear of others' adventures. Even Major Canfield, for all his attractiveness, thought women had no place following the drum or interfering in the rightful domain of men. Were he there to rescue her, as she had been weak enough to dream of on more than one drearily sleepless night, he would do no more than ship her straight home to England, to wait out the war in safety and inaction. And she had vowed to have done with leaving the heroics to others merely because of her gender.

Luckily her young protégé at last grew strong enough to move on, for she dared not leave him either there or with Father Gregorio when her own wedding took place. Father Gregorio reported afterward to her that he had successfully gotten him out under cover of darkness and sent him on his way south.

She had not even remonstrated with the old priest for his perfidy in revealing her plans to Don Ottavio. Nor, for his part, did he try to talk her out of her marriage. She knew he deplored her sacrifice, but he was as realistic as she, and realized she might soon have need of the French commandant's protection. For Don Ottavio, after that one outburst reminiscent of his old self, had sunk into a type of coma and could only now and then be roused to his senses. Neither believed he would live much longer. He had been far too weak to protect Reggie himself, but his reputation and her position as his stepdaughter had guarded her far more than he perhaps guessed. Without him, and without her imminent marriage to Monsieur de Thierry, she might indeed soon find herself at the mercy of the frightened French mob.

And it was bad enough as it was. As the days passed, and the threat of British attack grew more likely, the French in the town and even some of the Spanish who had collaborated with their French conquerors became more and more panic-stricken. The town itself was like a powder keg, ready to go off at the touch of a spark.

Reggie herself seldom ventured outside in those days, but Maria was able to bring her the rumors that the British had succeeded in outflanking the French army at Valladolid, who were now in a retreat that seemed perilously like a rout. The French had abandoned the line of the river Pisuerga and were falling back on Burgos yet again.

Most of the French in the town, many of whom had already fled from Madrid to Salamanca, then to Valladolid and now Burgos, desperately tried to hire, borrow, or steal whatever transportation they could manage to set out once more. It did not seem to occur to them that their ill-gotten plunder made each successive flight absurdly complicated, or that to transport ormolu clocks and bulky and expensive tapestries when they were in danger for their lives was ludicrous.

In fact, Reggie watched from her window one day as a French *fille de joie*, mistress, no doubt, of one of the French officers, bargained shrilly with an unimpressed and impassive Spanish peasant for the purchase of his farm cart, redolent of manure, to carry her expensive trunks filled with her chic gowns, jewels, and furs. She had sworn at him in French, expecting him to understand her and instantly fall in with her wishes, for she would lose everything—*every-*

thing! Did he not understand, the *bête d'Espagne*—and be ruined if she had to leave her things behind.

He had shrugged and gone on his way, and she had been left in the filthy street, with all her absurd and ultimately useless possessions piled around her, screaming abuse after him.

In the face of that, Reggie had refused to give in to complete despair. Events might yet save her, though she did not often allow herself to dream of such a convenient release. Were the city to come under British siege for the second time, there might be little enough time to think of bridals.

But it was a frail enough reed to cling to. Her common sense told her were that to happen she would be in little better shape and perhaps worse. Were the British to succeed this time, ten to one she would have long since been murdered by the French in the town, and in that case not even Monsieur de Thierry could save her.

The night before her wedding she sat up late, listening to the unrest outside in the warm darkness. The servants had all gone to bed, but the town itself was awake long after its accustomed hour. It seemed to simmer in a sullen silence that was every now and then broken by a shout, or the hasty sound of a carriage or heavy cart under the window. She had long since ceased wondering what was happening, for each piece of news only brought renewed alarm. But she knew she would not sleep, and it seemed little use to go through the charade of undressing.

Tomorrow she would face the French commandant at the altar and become his wife in a mockery of a service performed by her old friend, Father Gregorio. But it was no longer that she most feared. She had felt the tension build almost palpably outside her window for days now, and was aware of a terror, deep inside herself, that she had never experienced before. And so she sat up, her ears unconsciously straining in the dark, and her every muscle stiffened until she discovered even her jaw was aching with the tension.

Even as she tried, consciously, to relax it, there came the

sound outside that she had been subconsciously dreading for so long. Someone shouted a vile stream of abusive French, addressed directly at her, and then came the tinkle of broken glass as a brick or rock was hurled through the window near her.

She froze, her heart beginning to pound, knowing she had been a fool to sit up with the light on, pinpointing her location in the house. Even as she crouched there in her chair, wondering what to do, the voice outside was joined by still others, and another missile shattered a second window.

That at least unfroze her limbs, for clearly she could not just sit there waiting to be murdered, or worse. She wondered what had become of her French guards, but could not blame them for abandoning her in the face of a mob. But it meant that she alone was responsible for saving the other members of the household, and had only her own shaky wits and courage to sustain her.

Thoughts of giving herself up to the growing crowd outside in order to save the others were as abruptly abandoned. She did not need to see their faces to know that those below were animals, and that no one in the house would be safe from them. Certainly she would far better die by her own hand than risk their violence. She still had the little pistol Filipe had given her, and she reached quietly in the drawer beside her now and pulled it out, reassured by the cold of its steel.

Not that she could use it on herself until she had done what she could for the other members of the household. But even as she was wondering whether to go and awaken them, there came a new sound, this time unmistakably from within the house.

Her nerves screamed and sweat broke out all over her body as she waited in an agony of fear and dread, her hand tightening instinctively on the pistol. It might merely be one of the servants, wakened by the noise, coming to see if she was all right. But there was a decidedly furtive sound about it, as if someone crept up the staircase.

She turned slowly to face the door whence this new danger came. Shooting herself to escape the bestiality of the mob was one thing, but she had always doubted if she would have the courage to shoot another human being in cold blood. But in that moment she knew without question that she did. It seemed the French were not the only ones who could hate.

The stealthy sounds grew nearer. Below in the street, the shouting had continued, but she no longer heard it except as a backdrop to the furtive steps creeping toward the door behind which she stood. The light, too, must be visible beneath the doorsill, so that whoever was there would have no trouble in knowing in which room to find her. But it was too late to put out the candles, and she somehow feared even more finding herself in complete darkness with that dreadful menace just outside.

Then it was at the door. Her grip on the pistol was slippery by then and her hand shook woefully, so that she was unlikely to be able to hit anything in her present state. She must get a grip on herself. Slowly, slowly, the handle turned, and a thin line of darkness was revealed as the door was eased open.

She felt strangely light-headed, and there was no more room inside her head for the sound of anything but her own feverish heartbeat, but still she stood facing the door, the little pistol in her hand and pointed straight at the door, her finger tightening on the trigger even as the door swung wide.

Then in the next moment she had thrown the little pistol away and was in the newcomer's arms, laughing and crying all at the same time.

Chapter 17

IT WAS A long time before she could stop shuddering and find her voice. And when she did it was merely to gasp, "I thought—oh God! I almost killed you!"

"Hush. Hush now," said Adam, remarkably solid and real. "Anyway, I doubt you are as good a shot as that. I shall clearly have to teach you myself if you mean to continue your career as a spy." He still held her tightly in his arms, and sounded amazingly calm and normal.

Even as he spoke, another brick was launched through the window and landed in a hail of splintered glass almost at their feet. "But I think we can better carry on this conversation elsewhere." He spoke as calmly as if they had encountered each other in a ballroom, and did not have a murderous mob just outside the window. "This room would seem to be a little too public for my tastes."

She shuddered again as he led her quickly through the door he had just come through and onto the darker landing. "Oh, thank God you have come! But how did you—? Why—?"

"I have been worried about you, and just recently I have been unable to get you out of my mind. I should never have let you stay. And it would seem I arrived just in the nick of time. What in all the name that's holy has been going on here since last I saw you?"

She drew another ragged breath and passed over his somewhat remarkable assumption that he had any power over her movements. "Nothing. Everything. But the British army? Is it true they are going to attack Burgos?"

"Not only true, but they are not very far behind me. With any luck they'll be here by morning. I thought it would be better to get you out before the shooting started. But where is everyone else? Surely you are not alone in the house."

"No. Maria is about the place somewhere, and a few of the other servants, probably hiding their heads under their pillows. I can't blame them. But you—how did you manage to get in? Were there no guards at the door?"

"Not any that I saw," he informed her coolly, going to the end of the hall and investigating before opening another door and ushering her into a small parlor at the back of the house. "But I came in through the secret door. But where is your stepsister? And your stepfather? Surely they can't be sleeping through this."

She said unsteadily, having to blink back her useless tears, "Conchita is away on her honeymoon, I thank God. And Don Ottavio—Don Ottavio died last night."

He was beside her again swiftly. "My poor child. I'm sorry. But at least it makes things simpler. I should be shot for not insisting you leave the last time. But that is in the past. I hope you mean to advance no further foolish arguments to me about your duty, for I warn you, by hook or by crook, I am getting you out of here tonight."

So Filipe had been right. He had predicted that when the time came her major would have his way, brooking no protests. She found herself without so much as a single objection.

He seemed to find that amusing, for when she remained silent he added, "What, no protestations of equality? I feared you would still be bent on playing the determined heroine. What became of your fugitive, by the way? I hope I am not expected to get him out as well?"

She didn't even ask how he knew about that. She was beyond questioning miracles. "No, he has already left for Madrid. And if you want the truth, I haven't—felt much like a heroine, lately," she admitted wholeheartedly. "In fact, you can't know how relieved I am to see you."

"Thank God for that. And your fiancé? I understand congratulations are in order?"

He threw that out even more coolly, watching her with a steady regard that revealed nothing of his thoughts. He was again dressed as a Spanish peasant, but by now she was amazed that anyone would mistake him for a humble peasant. Certainly to her, in her present shattered state, he looked tough and capable and completely formidable. She would trust her life to him without a moment's hesitation.

She roused herself as if from a fog, and had to concentrate even to remember that other nightmare. Her wedding. Tomorrow. It seemed, thankfully, already another life. As another missile landed through a nearby window, she cried, "Oh God, there is not time for that now. Only get me out of here."

He actually laughed, looking suddenly unexpectedly carefree. "Well, that solves one of my problems, at least. Now there remains only one other. Let's hope I shall clear that as easily."

Then he straightened, abruptly looking every inch the military officer, accustomed to command, despite his shabby raiment. "But we'll leave that for the moment. There is not a second to be wasted. Change quickly into whatever dark and sturdy clothes you can find, and bring a dark cloak. Leave everything else behind. We must travel light, and there will be no room for baggage, I'm afraid. Where is your henchwoman, the stout and forbidding Maria? If she is to accompany you, she must be prepared to move quickly."

"I will ask her, of course," she said unsteadily, a little bemused by the rapidity with which everything had changed. The dark cloud under which she had existed for so long seemed miraculously to have lifted, and she was almost giddy with the relief of it. "But I suspect she will prefer to remain behind. Her husband is here, you know, and her children."

He was frowning. "Very well. I confess it will make the immediate future easier, for we still have the gates to get through safely, and the fewer of us there are the better. Now, go and get ready. And wear comfortable shoes, for I fear we will have some walking ahead of us."

She did as he bid, asking no more questions. It was enough that he was there. The future could take care of itself, though she had no notion at the moment what that future might be. Whether—but it was past time for speculation, or even useless considerations of propriety. For the moment she was content to leave everything in Adam's very capable hands. She had known fear and heartache, and had no promise of anything different in the future. But for all her recent terror, it was still far better than sitting safely in England doing her embroidery.

She was back in a remarkably short space of time, attired in one of Conchita's severe black dresses, and wrapped in an enveloping cloak. She had stopped to tie only a few necessary items in a shawl, and was leaving behind all her possessions and her old familiar life without a qualm. Maria had promised to see Don Ottavio decently buried, as well as getting word, God willing, to Conchita and Filipe as to what had happened to her.

Adam greeted her on her return as calmly as if no enemy army and possibly enraged mob stood between them and safety. "Good! I am glad to see you took me at my word and brought little with you."

"My dear Major," she said in amusement, "I was just reflecting before you came on how foolish the French were to try to save their possessions when their very lives were in danger. I believe I can do without a few keepsakes and changes of clothes."

"Good girl!" His approval warmed her absurdly. "But it is no longer 'Major.' My promotion came through in the spring. Now, I have only one more stop to make, and then we can be away."

She wondered what that could be, but asked no questions. As they made their way safely out the secret door, evading the unpleasant mob, she reflected a little dazedly on how quickly everything could change. From being paralyzed with terror, she now knew an odd buoyancy, as if some great new adventure were just beginning.

Away from her house there were still a number of people on the streets seeking shelter or searching for transportation or reassurance. Reggie was grateful for her cloak, with its enveloping and disguising hood, but Adam, in his present attire, moved confidently, as if he were not an English soldier who would be shot on sight if discovered there.

The thought made her shiver, but she quickly rejected it. They had seen no guards outside the house, which fact raised brief indignation in her. So much for Monsieur de Thierry's protection!

That thought briefly recalled her erstwhile fiancé to her, and she knew a brief moment's guilt. He had been kind to her in his own way, and deserved better than to be jilted without a word of explanation. But then, if Adam was right, he would have far more on his mind tomorrow than a wedding.

It took her a moment to realize that Adam had led her in a roundabout way to the church. She could only suppose he had some business with Father Gregorio, and was glad enough to be able to bid that kindly cleric goodbye.

They found the priest in rapt meditation, but he looked up quickly at their appearance and, crossing himself, rose immediately. "Good, you have brought her," he surprised Reggie very much by saying. "All is well, my son?"

Adam grinned. "Very well, Father."

Reggie found herself clinging to the old priest's worn hands. "It seems I must go, Father," she managed. "Will you be safe?"

"You need not concern yourself with me, my child," he

said serenely. "It is in the hands of God, as all things are. It was clearly God himself who sent this one here to save you. You have done more than was expected of you. It is best to go now and leave it in other hands."

Her grip briefly tightened. "And—Don Ottavio?"

"He is with God now, and beyond need of your concern. Rest assured I will see all is done as it should be and see to his proper burial. May God protect his soul."

"Much as I am loath to end these leavetakings, we have very little time, I'm afraid," Adam interrupted. "Father, you will do as I requested?"

"Assuredly, my son."

Adam's grin flashed in the dim light. "Then, you will marry us now?" he said astonishingly. "We must be out of here as soon as possible."

Reggie froze. Even her breath seemed suspended. "*What* did you say?"

"Gently, gently, my dear," said Colonel Canfield, with a quick glance at the priest. "But are you surprised? I have been continually frustrated by having no right to protect you. I have no intention of that happening again. I will have you safely tied to me before we move a foot."

"He is right, my child," put in Father Gregorio earnestly. "I could not forbid you to go with him, but I confess I was troubled. This will make it all right."

She looked from one to the other, and saw that, manlike, they had arranged it all between themselves without even thinking of consulting her. They could not have expressed their thoughts more clearly: women were but a nuisance in any emergency, and to be dealt with as they had always been; pacified, silenced, and then forgotten while men went about the important work of war.

And it did not matter that her heart had quite definitely leaped for one betraying instant, or that what he offered so casually had long represented the sum of her dreams.

She asked quietly, "And once we are safely wed you will

waste no time in shipping me back to England to your relations, is that right?"

"I only wish it were in my power," he said ruefully. "The chances are high we will be in battle soon—perhaps the most decisive of the war. Unfortunately, I've not time to send you to the rear, and no one I dare trust to escort you. I'm afraid you will have no choice but to join the army, at least for the time being. It is hardly an ideal solution, for you will find it very different from the life you are used to. In fact, if I could think of any other way, believe me, I would."

Every word he said was a death knell to her hopes. But she made herself say with some irony, "In the face of my present alternatives, do you really think I will consider a little inconvenience? At any rate, there are other women with the army. Presumably they do not find it too unpleasant."

"Yes, most of them rough creatures who take a new husband every time their present one is killed," he said impatiently. "But this is hardly the time for such a discussion. And Father Gregorio is waiting."

He had given her her answer without any further room for doubt or foolish hope. Nothing had changed. Whatever his feelings toward her—and she was very far from knowing what they were even yet—he felt a responsibility toward her. The marriage was simply a sop to convention, for he could scarcely take her back with him otherwise. As soon as he was able he would ship her back to Madrid, or now probably London, and no doubt be relieved to have gotten so lightly out of the affair.

Certainly he still had no understanding or desire for the sort of marriage she yearned after: two partners sharing both the troubles and the joys of life together. A working partnership, and a need for each other so great that it outweighed all considerations of convention or safety.

She was right back where she had started from, almost a year ago. Nothing had changed with a vengeance, except that now he offered her the unwilling protection of his name, as in honor bound.

She knew her own recent experiences should have made her leap at what he offered, no matter how little it was. If nothing else, he offered safety and even some form of commitment. Doubtless, to his way of thinking, it would limit him little enough to have a wife back in England, at least so long as the war continued. And in return she would have a respectable position and could make some form of a life of her own. Certainly when looked at in exchange for the marriage she had been contemplating that day, it was heaven indeed.

And yet. And yet. Two fatal little words. For he had uttered not one word about love. It was, perhaps, scarcely the time, but still, the omission was more than significant. She was foolish enough to still be longing for the return of moonbeams, when what he offered was a simple and indeed generous solution to her difficulties. She was doubtless churlish in the extreme to see it as but a small, a pitifully small part of what she wanted.

"So that you can get back to more important duties, is that it?" she asked more quietly still.

Something in her tone finally got to him. "What? What the devil are you talking about?"

She took a deep breath, victory tasting oddly like ashes in her mouth. "Never mind. I will marry you tonight," she said tiredly. "But on one condition. That we have the marriage annulled as soon as possible. Having avoided one expedient marriage this day, I find no stomach to undertake another."

Chapter 18

ADAM GLANCED at the priest, who since they had been speaking in English was blissfully unaware of what was being said. Then he grabbed her arm urgently and pulled her a little way apart. "Perhaps you will explain to me what the sweet hell is going through that exasperating head of yours now?" he demanded dangerously. "I thought we had done with protests. Or do you really imagine this is no more than an attempt to force you into something for my own ends?"

That was almost ironic, but she refused to be bullied. "No, it would seem it is rather I who am forcing you into something you have no desire for."

That got him. He said something extremely profane under his breath, and glanced again at the still smiling priest. Then with unflattering abruptness he gave in. "Very well. There is not time to argue anything at the moment, for in case you have forgotten, we must still get out of this damn place. And there is no other solution. If there were don't you think I would take it? I have no more liking for this hole in the corner affair than you do. But I won't easily forgive myself for allowing you to come back the last time. It is my fault you have had to endure all that you have."

There was her answer, if she needed any more proof. She found herself oddly near to weak, foolish tears and had to fight them back, despising the feminine folly. "And women and children have no place in war. You have made your views on that subject very clear."

She spoke almost drearily, and he glanced sharply at her again. But there was indeed no time. The priest was growing uneasy, and the horrors of the town still lay without. He swore abruptly again, then raised his voice. "Yes, we're coming, Father. Look," he said impatiently to her again, lowering his voice. "I may have handled this badly. I daresay I have. But it scarcely seems the moment for romantic declarations. Do you want me to apologize for the last time we met? I won't. I confess I thoroughly enjoyed it—at least parts of it—and wouldn't give it up for a fortune. Are you angry because I made no declaration then? Is that what this is about? Because if so, you don't have to beat me up for that, sweetheart. I have beaten myself up a hundred times since. If it is any comfort to you, I have paid more than I think you can imagine for that failure. But that is neither here nor there. I was right at the time to mistrust what was between us. We had met in highly romantic circumstances, to say the least, and I have lived too long with war not to know how dangerous that can be."

As usual, things were rapidly getting out of hand, but she was inclined to be indignant that he could think she was sulking merely because he hadn't made love to her. "And what makes this any different?" she demanded almost childishly.

He actually laughed. "What makes this different is that neither one of us any longer has a choice. Besides, I have discovered that being sensible doesn't get you out of my head or my heart. It seems you will continue to haunt me, whatever I do. And that being the case, I intend this time to have you where I can keep an eye on you at least until I can send you safely back to England."

It always came back to that. "You still persist in seeing me as some slightly foolish child who must be saved from the consequences of her own folly. Very well! I concede it. I ruined everything, and forced you into this dramatic rescue. But I won't make things even worse by forcing you into marriage as well. At least we will go through a mockery, for form's sake, but that's all it will be."

He gathered her hands and held them tightly, despite her resistance. "Hell and the devil confound it! Darling, I know I've made a muck of this and put your back up. But you know as well as I do that there is something between us. More, our futures seem to be inextricably linked somehow. Whether that's enough to base a marriage on, I honestly don't know. I've never been married before. I only know that I want the right to protect you, and if that's not romantic enough for you, I'm sorry. But we are rather pressed at the moment, and besides, we have a witness in the shape of the good friar here."

"And even more important, you have a war to fight!" she said even more childishly.

To her extreme annoyance he was openly laughing now. "Yes, I have a war to fight. And that is another reason I agree to your terms—for the moment. Good Lord, you little fool, did you really think I would hold a gun to your head to marry me in this absurd fashion and then immediately carry you off to my bed? It seems to me your opinions of men are as unflattering as you seem to think mine are of women. When I make love to you—and I have been looking forward to that almost since the moment I met you—I promise you it won't be on the eve of battle, or in a cramped tent. You are at least right about one thing. A campaign is no time to be engaging in a honeymoon, much as I might long to. If nothing else, I have no idea how long it may be before I can get you to safety, and you might become pregnant."

She should have known she could never get the better of him. She was blushing furiously by then. "That wasn't what I meant, and you know it."

He sobered then. "No, I know. But whatever you or I might wish, sweetheart, this curst war must come first. Afterward—but at the moment I think neither of us can even think beyond that. And until and if it is over, private feel-

ings must be sacrificed. That is always the way in wartime,
I'm afraid."

She wondered if he even wanted it differently. She had
seen too much of Filipe to know the joy he got from his
odd life to ever imagine him marrying and settling down.
She said abruptly, annoyed with herself for having precipi-
tated such a scene, "This is getting us nowhere. But whatever happens, I make no promises of agreeing to be shipped
off, like so much baggage, when it should become convenient to you. I may be marrying you, but I am not giving up
a whit of my independence. Is that understood?"

He laughed again. "How could I forget it? And remind
me to tell you, when it is rather more convenient, that you
are a darling, Miss Regina Alderstock, soon to be Canfield.
And it had better be soon, I fear. This is neither the time
nor the place for any of this. I suggest we leave it till later
and allow the good friar to marry us, so that we can get out
of here before all hell breaks loose."

And so they were married, in a dim church lit only by a
few candles, the sexton hurriedly summoned as a witness.
The priest was hurried but relieved, as if he did not recognize the sham that this marriage was, and Reggie thought it
was just as well. She had no desire to disillusion him with
the truth that he joined in holy wedlock, in such simple and
beaming joy, a soldier who had no desire to be saddled with
a wife, and a woman who had but one steadfast thought
throughout. That she would rather die than become a mill-
stone round his neck, or seem to demand anything from
him that he was not fully prepared to give.

Even so, it was a more moving ceremony than she would
have expected. The ancient cathedral was beautiful and familiar to her, and the yellow glow of the few candles en-
closed them in a strange and unexpected intimacy.
Moreover, the elderly priest who spoke the lines in his
deep, loving voice did not appear to realize this marriage
had no meaning for either of them. Nor did he seem to re-

member that danger lay just outside the door, and it was no certainty any of them would escape with their lives.

Reggie, standing in something of a dream, that earlier horror still at the corners of her consciousness and too aware of the strong grasp on her hand of the stranger she was marrying, could not help but contrast this with the wedding she had thought to undergo on the morrow. At the thought she shivered a little and at once Adam's hand tightened on hers.

It occurred to her then, hearing the beautiful, ancient words, that she was no longer certain this wouldn't be the way she would have chosen to be married after all. The attendants and lace veils of her imaginings, and that had been so much in evidence at Conchita's recent marriage, now seemed unreal, and this simple ceremony, in the dark, and performed by an old friend, was suddenly far more right to her than Conchita's stiff and formal affair.

But it was dangerous to think that way. She repeated her vows in a clear voice, and heard Adam answer in the same, his hand still strong and warm on hers.

Only when the end came, and Father Gregorio, in his simplicity, said with touching happiness in his old voice, "You may now kiss the bride," did she give a little gasp, and waken, as from a dream.

Adam was looking at her, a question in his eyes. If only for the reason that she wanted it so much, she knew she should have refused to take part in this final mockery. But for Father Gregorio's sake she mutely lifted her face for his kiss.

And yet, when his lips touched hers it was curiously hard to remember that this ceremony was but a mockery, and war awaited them just outside the door. It almost seemed as if Adam trembled, too; certainly his hand tightened on hers almost to the point of pain, and he was breathing rather hard. For her own part, her thoughts whirled and broke apart, and the danger, the mockery of a ceremony, the necessity to remember it meant less than nothing, all whirled away with it.

It was over far too soon, and she had to struggle with her sharp disappointment. Father Gregorio and the sexton were congratulating them, and she found she was still clinging to Adam's hand, as if she feared she would float away without his anchoring her to the ancient, dusty floor she stood on.

She accepted the warm congratulations, telling herself blankly that they were married. It had really happened. And yet it was no true marriage, for it meant nothing to either of them, and she must not let herself forget that. Even more to the point, outside the door lay all the horror and danger she had momentarily forgotten, and the grief of Don Ottavio's death. It was foolish in the extreme to allow herself to float away on sentimental dreams when they had still to get out of town, and might both be dead or arrested by tomorrow. It was more than time she pulled herself together and faced reality.

After that sharp lecture to herself, she was able to sign her name calmly enough in the church registry, and pull her mind back to mundane matters. Father Gregorio promised to get word to Filipe if he came again, and to pass on when possible her note to Conchita. There was still Don Ottavio's burial to think of, and it was impossible to say, under the present circumstances, when that might take place.

Only then did it strike her that for that matter she had no idea when, or even if, she would see any of them again. But it was past time to consider that, and she had been more than foolish enough already. She would not further disgrace herself by breaking down completely before her new husband.

Her husband, her husband, her husband. The words kept echoing in her head. She had to shake them away, for if one thing were more certain than the next, in what had become a very uncertain world, it was that she could not afford to depend too much on Colonel Adam Canfield. From the first, circumstances had thrown them into an unnatural intimacy, and it was true that at the moment he seemed a rock to cling to in her all-too-crumbling world. But in a very few weeks she would be on her own again, and she had the feeling that if she ever let down, after all the years she had had no one but her own strength to rely on, she might fall apart completely. And that would be a final humiliation she could not afford.

The trip through the town was one of the strangest experiences Reggie had in that night of remarkable events. Though it was well past midnight, most of the town seemed to be out in the streets, milling around in panic. The fear was tangible and the only good thing was that no one seemed to pay them any attention at all in that throng. She had been prepared for a silent and nerve-racking journey through the sleeping town, fearing at any moment to be discovered by French soldiers. Instead she discovered they could make their way quite boldly, with no need to hide or cower in dark corners.

In fact, it quickly became apparent that most of the French were out in the streets, trying to beg, borrow, or steal transport. A *fille de chambre*, in hysterics, accosted them to demand they help her escape, or else hide her before the English came to murder her in her bed. Her mistress, she claimed, had abandoned her, and she had no idea where to turn.

They were forced to leave her behind, of course, though Reggie was troubled by her obvious terror. She had herself become too familiar with terror in the last few days to dismiss it easily in anyone else.

Another stout French gentleman of obvious wealth stopped to demand of them if they had transport of any kind, even mules. He must get his family out in safety and would pay any price.

They shook their heads and hurried on, Reggie gratefully clinging to Adam's arm. They saw few French soldiers of any kind, and none paid them any attention. The whole town seemed to have gone mad, and though it was primarily the French that were reacting in panic, a number of Spanish were in the streets as well, either to discover what they could, or to make shrewd bargains, selling the most decrepit of vehicles and broken-down mules at unconscionable prices, or buying the luxuries of the French, some of whom seemed to be jettisoning everything in their panic.

Reggie found herself grateful to follow in Adam's large and purposeful wake. At first she had kept her head lowered and her hood well down, fearing to be recognized. But she quickly saw that that was an unnecessary precaution. No one was interested in her any longer.

Adam spoke only when absolutely necessary, saying once to her, when they were caught up in a mob of panicked French, "Don't stop. Keep moving!" And then again, when they at last neared the gates, "This is the tricky part. Keep your face covered and leave everything to me."

She nodded, aware that her heart had begun to hammer in a disconcerting way in her breast and that she was far more breathless than the fast walk through the town warranted.

But to her astonishment, the gates of the town were standing wide. It would seem the guards had abandoned any attempt to control the traffic in and out. Most of it was out, a steady stream of French, in whatever conveyance they had managed to find, loaded with as many of their worldly goods as they could pile on, and all with grim and strained faces. Many of them held firearms ready to ward off the importunate or more determined attempts to commandeer their vehicles, and all of them looked stunned, as if they could scarcely believe this was happening to them.

Reggie said incredulously, under cover of the din, "They are abandoning the city!"

"Yes. I thought earlier that was what was happening. It may just be panic, or something more. It makes it even more important that I get back quickly, for I must report what's going on. Let's hope no one finds where I left my horse, for we won't find another in this madhouse and it's a long walk otherwise. Keep your head down in case anyone recognizes you, but I think we're safe enough."

She did as he bid, feeling her heart still hammering unpleasantly. They actually had to push and jostle their way through the gates, but no one glanced at them, except to curse them or try to push them out of the way. She had never been a part of such panic, and it straightened her own spine, for such abject flight in the face of no more than rumors stirred her complete contempt.

So it was that she was able to stroll out of the town calmly, with no more than a glance back at the place that had been her home for so long. She spared one brief thought to the marriage that was to have taken place tomorrow, and could not imagine now how she had steeled herself to it. It was already so far in the past it seemed like nothing so much as a nightmare from which she had thankfully awakened in time.

Surprisingly, it was Adam who seemed worried now. "Damn! This is the one thing I had not counted on. I fear we have a mile or more to go, and even then I can't guarantee that the horse I left will still be there. Can you bear to hurry just a little?"

She lifted her chin, completely calm now. "Good God, don't worry about me. You set the pace and I will contrive to keep up."

Even so she suspected he adjusted his long stride to fit her shorter one, and one moreover hampered with the inconvenience of petticoats. For the first time she cursed herself for not having had the forethought to put on some of Filipe's clothes, for it seemed to her that that would have solved all their problems. Certainly that sham marriage might not have had to take place.

Then she had to laugh silently and a little hysterically at such uncharacteristic flights into the realm of fiction. She would not wager any odds on her being able to keep up such a disguise, even for a day or two, and the scandal once she was discovered would be far greater than merely appearing in the ranks under Adam's protection. It galled her to admit it, but Father Gregorio and Adam had been right. In neither case would her reputation long survive; and though at the moment it seemed absurd to worry about such things, when her very life was threatened, she was sensible enough to know that once safe it would loom very large again—especially if lost completely.

Adam had soon enough plunged off the main road, still crowded with refugees, and though she was thankful to leave them behind, it made walking very much more difficult. It seemed to her they walked for miles in the dark, and though she would have died rather than complain, she was very soon breathless and feared at every step to wrench her ankle on the uneven ground. She was soon cursing her hampering skirts in earnest, for she had never felt more useless or more annoyingly dependent.

Adam, for his part, seemed to cover the ground tirelessly, his strong arm supporting her over the uneven ground, and stopping and waiting every little while for her to catch her breath. It seemed resentfully to her that he could see like a cat in the dark, for he did not hesitate, while she, who had ridden every inch of the surrounding countryside, was soon hopelessly lost. There was very little moon, and even the stars were covered, so that she feared it would rain later. At any event, the dark made everything different, so that she was no longer even sure of directions, and had to rely upon him completely.

She said once, breathlessly, "Blast you! I fear for all my boasting I am but a sore burden to you. How did you see that patch of gorse that I just stumbled into?"

He laughed. "I have been this way before, remember. And you're doing very well. I confess I feared I would have to carry you this last way—and doubtless with any other woman I would have. As usual, you confound all my prejudices."

She was warmed a little by his praise, and straightened her aching spine again. But though she made no complaint, it seemed galling to her that she was very much a handicap to him. Moreover she knew he was anxious to return to his regiment and deliver his urgent message.

But at the least the need for haste to deliver his message was soon taken abruptly from them. They had gone little more than a mile from town when the night was shattered by a deafening explosion that suddenly turned the darkness into a dazzling light.

Chapter 19

IT WAS FOLLOWED more slowly by a thunder that seemed to rend the night apart and leave Reggie deaf and staggering. They were a good mile or more distant, and yet so great was the noise and light that she felt battered by it, and would have fallen had not Adam's strong arm been there, and he grasped her tightly, supporting her.

When she could speak again she cried in a sudden terror, "What was it? Has the whole town blown up?"

"No, no. The explosion was not big enough, and centered in one part only," he reassured her. "Unless I miss my guess I would say the French have exploded the castle, with all its munitions. And if so they are in a panic, for they have not cleared the town yet. But if I know his lordship, that is all the signal he needs. Sweetheart, I'm extremely sorry to be obliged to push you any more, especially since you have been such a trooper already, but unless we make haste we may miss them completely. Wellington won't stay for anything now. But I promise you it's not much further."

She had thought they were already going as fast as they could, but she soon learned she was mistaken. His strong arm under hers urged her on, and in the face of his confidence in her she would not admit that she was near to flagging, that she had somehow wrenched her ankle someway back and it was beginning to pain her, or that even her sensible shoes seemed to be little protection against the rough ground they were covering so speedily. She feared her feet were being painfully bruised, but would have seen them cut to the bone before holding him back any further. She had her pride, after all.

But she was beyond relief when she heard the comforting whicker of a horse in the warm darkness. She gladly increased her speed, and it was only as they reached the solitary animal tethered to a stunted tree, and cropping peacefully, that the significance hit her.

She stopped and said on a gasp, which was all the breath she had remaining, "One horse! You did not mean to bring me back with you."

"I meant to if I could," he said calmly, and to her great resentment sounding scarcely winded. "But I left in such a hurry there was no time to borrow a sidesaddle for you. You will be comfortable enough up before me, and Rodrigo here can easily carry both of us."

He was busy at his saddle as he spoke, and had unstrapped a heavy boat cloak, which he shook out and insisted upon wrapping around her. "It looks like rain, and I fear you will be cold, but there's no help for it, I'm sorry to say. But you have done the worst of it. The rest will be easy by comparison, I promise you."

He was still treating her like a fine piece of porcelain to be protected, but she unwillingly knew herself to be a lamentable handicap to him at the moment. He had at the beginning of that strange and breathless journey relieved her of the shawl containing her few things, and now proceeded to strap it on in the cloak's place. "Now up with you," he said firmly, and lifted her into the saddle.

She had the impression, admittedly not unpleasant, of being as light as a feather and having had all decisions taken out of her hands. Later she would doubtless be resentful, but for the moment she was too weary to care, nor had she the breath left to protest.

He quickly swung himself up behind her and took the reins, and set off at a rapid pace that soon had her grateful for the security of his arms. Indeed, she soon discovered she was surprisingly comfortable and wrapped in warmth.

It was a sensation she had never experienced before, being held so closely in a man's embrace, so that she could feel his chest rising and falling and his light breath on her hair.

Or rather, she had experienced it, as a child held tight in her father's arms. Some of the same sense of security and safety crept over her, and despite the many alarms of the night, despite her weariness in every bone and her lacerated feet, despite the gamut of emotions she had been through in the past few days, she found her eyes drooping. She forced them up once or twice, but it was a losing proposition. To her own vast astonishment, she soon slept.

She roused once to find her cheek snug on his rough jacket, and his heart beating steadily in her ear. Immensely comforted, she drifted off again. Later still she found that it had begun to rain, but she was snug in his boat cloak, and protected, and it did not much disturb her. She did rouse enough to realize that he was getting steadily soaked, and tried to protest, but even to herself her words made little sense.

He glanced down at her, as if amused, the rain dripping off his hat and the cloak under her cheek uncomfortably damp. "Never mind about me, I'm used to the wet," he said calmly. "Are you warm enough?"

"Oh, so warm," she murmured sleepily.

She felt his chest move under her, as if he were laughing about something, and she thought she heard him say under his breath, "At last! It is remarkable what fear and a sleepless night can do, even to the starchy and independent Miss Alderstock. But I have a feeling I had best enjoy this while it lasts, for I doubt this sudden docility." She thought his arms tightened around her and he dropped a quick kiss on her hair, but she was already asleep again even as the impression occurred.

Later she roused to protest again, "I am too heavy for you, and you are so wet."

"You are—just right," he said, and his voice sounded

close to her ear and remarkably cheerful. "Now go back to sleep. It won't be long now."

Incredibly, she snuggled more closely against him and did drift gratefully back to sleep, thinking confusedly that as a wedding night, it was an undoubtedly odd one, but she was not sure she would have changed it for anything.

Afterward she was to realize they must have made excellent time, despite the double load on his horse, for they reached the main body of the British army just as it was breaking up camp before first light. She woke properly at the first sound of voices, to find Adam had stopped to inquire after news of the first troops they encountered.

A young lieutenant scarcely old enough to shave yet assured him eagerly that they had indeed all been wakened by the explosions, and were under orders to march in the next hour. Rumor had it they were to cross the Ebro in pursuit of the French.

Adam whistled, but made no other comment except to thank his informer. But when he had moved on again, in search of his regiment, and saw that she was awake, he commented, "I had a suspicion that's what his lordship would be up to. It's risky, and I don't doubt he's alarmed a good many of his senior officers, but I'd do the same. We've already got them on the retreat now."

She stretched her stiff body, aware of a certain belated embarrassment in remembering how she had slept on him last night. So much for her notions of an impersonal marriage of convenience! But she said now, anxiously, "You mean we are to follow them into France?"

"With any luck. Or at least out of Spain. We've got them rompéd, if I'm any judge. They wouldn't have abandoned Burgos if they weren't hopelessly shattered. By God, it's the best news I've heard in a long while!"

She looked up into his face, and saw him grinning with excitement. She recognized the same reckless happiness she had often seen in her stepbrother's face when he was off on some dangerous mission, and reflected ruefully that for all her wishing, there still lay an unconquerable gap between the sexes. The thought of battle could not help but fill her with dismay, but that was obviously the last thought in Adam's mind.

Dismay was clearly absent from the rest of the army as well, as she quickly came to realize. They found his regiment cheerfully stamping out their fires and loading up the tents and canteens, and Adam and Reggie both came in for a good deal of amazed greeting. The men stared at her as if they had never seen a woman before, and Adam's friends and fellow officers hurried out to roast him for nearly holding them up.

They were far more adept at hiding their feelings than their men at the sight of her, and if they felt any dismay at having her foisted upon the army, they admirably concealed it. Her own particular acquaintance greeted her with flattering warmth and merely expressed relief that she had been rescued. Still, it was an awkward enough moment, and one she had been dreading.

But in the event it passed off more easily than she had expected. There was clearly little time for delay, and Adam commended her to Captain Prescott's care, saying hurriedly, "Be a good fellow, Suttler, and take care of her for me. I must see to some sort of transport for her immediately. I'll explain everything when I get back. In the meantime, find something for her to eat and a cup of strong tea, and I'll be back shortly."

She found herself a little shy once Adam had gone, but soon recovered under Captain Prescott's calm cheerfulness. He escorted her to his tent, not yet struck, and yelled for his batman to fetch her a cup of tea and find her something to eat. When she protested that it was not necessary, he assured her they had plenty of time yet, for they were not under orders for nearly an hour.

That seemed little enough time to her, given all the confusion she saw around her. But she was soon to learn that the confusion always sorted itself out into remarkable efficiency, in some mysterious and miraculous way. During her hasty meal of eggs and ham, which tasted ambrosial to her after her long night, Captain Prescott regaled her with amusing anecdotes of their winter quarters, which he described as being unfit for men or animals, and all that had happened since he saw her last.

He asked her no questions, but she was aware that behind his pleasant gaze there was a certain speculation which she found herself quite unable to satisfy.

In fact, in the light of that calm, early June morning last night's exploits began to seem more and more incredible even to her. Had that hurried marriage really taken place? It seemed more and more unlikely.

Then Adam returned, looking remarkably cheerful for all his sleepless night, and sanity returned once more for her. He was bearing a habit he had managed to unearth from somewhere and a pair of boots, and armed with the information that he had found her a ride in one of the generals' wives' carriage.

He, too, wolfed down a quick breakfast, describing for his friend the panic he had seen in the streets of Burgos, and speculating with him on Wellington's likely plans. Both seemed eager to catch up with the French, and spared not a thought for any possible danger.

Still no mention had been made of that hasty marriage. But just when Reggie was beginning to relax, Adam confounded her by adding calmly, "By the way, thank you for looking after her for me, Suttler. You shall be the first to congratulate me. We were married last night."

Captain Prescott did not choke over his coffee, and she saw that from his reaction he must already have come to that conclusion. "I do congratulate you!" he said warmly, his ugly face lighting up. "In fact, you have stolen a march on me, you dog. And on a number of others I could name. We must have a party to celebrate as soon as we are able."

Adam grinned, seemingly in no whit embarrassed. "God knows when that will be! I do pick my moments don't I?

But by God, this time I really think we have them on the run!"

And they were off, well launched into that man's world where she couldn't hope to follow. She had to bite back a sudden sharp stab of jealousy as unworthy as it was ridiculous.

But in truth, talk of a party seemed more unreal to Reggie at the moment; almost as unreal as that hurried midnight ceremony. For even as they spoke the call to arms was sounded, and the men began to form up.

Adam still had to change into his uniform and report back in, so Captain Prescott was deputized to escort Reggie to her transport. Their goodbye was thus hasty and far from private.

But there was little to say after all. She said inadequately, "I—when will I see you again?"

He grinned down at her and took her hands in his large warm ones. "Don't worry. I'll find you when we stop, and probably before that. Mrs. Delafield will take care of you. She's a seasoned campaigner. We're in for an uncomfortable march, I fear, but you should be able to doze in her carriage. You got very little sleep last night I know."

She longed to point out that he had had none. He looked very different from the elegant officer at the ball, so long ago in Madrid. He needed a shave, and was still in his disreputable Spanish peasant clothes, and only the twinkle in his blue eyes and infectious grin were recognizable.

He smiled at her again and squeezed her hand. "Don't worry about anything, sweetheart," he said. "It will all work out somehow."

She was not even surprised to see that he was in tearing spirits. She had the evidence all around her of how eager the entire army was to come to grips with the enemy, whatever the danger.

Clearly it behooved her to betray none of her own churning emotions. She said equally as calmly, "Yes. Don't worry about me."

She was rewarded by his quick smile again. "Now I really must go, I'm afraid. I'll see you tonight." Unexpectedly he raised one of the hands he held to his lips. Then a brief salute and he was gone.

As Captain Prescott escorted her toward the rear, Reggie told herself sharply that if she were to be undone by every such careless gesture, she stood not a chance in this sham of a marriage of theirs. But even so her hand tingled from the touch of his lips long afterward.

She looked at her calm escort, and said inadequately, "You must wonder—I daresay you must think so—so precipitate a marriage outrageous, Captain."

Captain Prescott grinned, "Lord no! I've stopped being surprised at anything Adam does. I'm only sorry he stole such a march on the rest of them. Trust Adam to seize his opportunities. Though I'll admit the rest of them will be likely to roast him unmercifully. You must know, my dear Mrs. Canfield, that until now his views on the inadvisability of women following the drum have been well known. He'll never hear the last of this."

She stared at this first use of her married name, acknowledging hollowly that his words were all it had needed to make her morning complete.

Chapter 20

MRS. DELAFIELD proved to be a stout, weathered-looking creature of sixty or so, with a calm manner and a pleasant greeting. It was plain that Adam had told her a little of Reggie's history, for she expressed astonishment that they had been married the night before, in a French-occupied town, and was eager to hear the whole story.

It was, Reggie knew, but the beginning of what she feared would be a nine-days' wonder amongst Adam's friends. Mrs. Delafield exclaimed over her tale, but soon said kindly, "And now you must be exhausted. Don't think you have to chat with me, my dear. I am quite used to being alone."

And so Reggie, who despite her naps from the night before was indeed exhausted, settled herself in one corner and tried to sleep. But the newness of the experience, the awkwardness of her present situation, and the noise and confusion all around her easily defeated her purpose.

Very soon there was another reason as well. Mrs. Delafield's carriage, though comfortable enough, traveled with the baggage train at the rear, and Reggie soon discovered that that was a far from enviable position. At the first their wheels had been mired in mud from the storm of the night before, but as the sun came out with all its summer fierceness and quickly dried the road, the advancing army kicked up such a dust storm that it almost seemed as if the sun had been blotted out and they were in a cloud of red dirt. The red dust seeped through the tightly closed windows of the coach and seemed to penetrate everywhere, so that by the end of the day Reggie felt as if she had grit in every fold of her clothing and even down to her skin.

Their choice seemed to be either to close all the windows tight against the choking dust, and swelter in the increasing heat, or to open the windows and cough. Mrs. Delafield chose to swelter, and Reggie, though inured to the heat after having lived in it for so long, soon found herself near to fainting.

More than that, their progress was so slow that she was strongly tempted at times to get out and walk instead. It would have been a relief from the heat and the tedium. And the carriage, struggling first through mud, then through the baked ruts left by earlier traffic, left her black and blue.

She soon gave up entirely on the idea of sleep and whiled away the time watching the ever-changing show around her. It was indeed a town, and a large one, on the move, for aside from the interminable columns of marching men in shabby red uniforms, some of them so shapeless or mended that they scarcely resembled a uniform at all, there was the enormous baggage train, cluttered up with camp followers, most of them the rough wives and mistresses of the common troopers, wagons loaded with ammunition and stores, and herds of goats and horses shepherded by swarms of half-grown Portuguese boys.

Adam had sent his groom, Hanson, to introduce himself and keep an eye on her, and if he thought it odd his master should have taken a wife in so hurried a fashion, after all his stated prejudice against wives cluttering up the army, he was careful to keep a noncommittal expression fixed firmly on his face. He merely touched his hat to her and said stolidly, "The colonel's compliments, ma'am, and he will see you this evening, when we bivouac. He regrets he won't be able to see you before then, for he has his duties to attend to."

She suspected that Hanson, too, shared his master's view on women in the tail of the army, and said promptly, "Indeed, assure him for me, if you see him, that I am very well, and expect nothing from him. I would not have him neglect his duty for the world. As for you, you, too, must have your duties as well, and no time to be dancing attendance on me. Pray go about them as usual, for I am being very well looked-after."

Hanson thawed slightly, and taking her at her word, presently took himself off again. Mrs. Delafield had already warned her that an officer's groom was highly important to him, for an army on the move never knew when it would encounter the enemy and perhaps find itself in battle, and the spare horses kept by his groom could be vital if his mount should be shot from under him.

Reggie shivered a little at this unnecessary reminder of the proximity of the French. More, it seemed strange, after living so long among them, to find herself with the British army instead. Not that it wasn't a most reassuring and welcome change.

By the time they called a halt at last, in the late afternoon, her eyes were red, her stamina exhausted, and she wanted to do nothing but to crawl into her bed and sleep for a week. And she had done nothing but sit in a carriage all day. She hesitated to think what the troops, who had trudged all that weary way, must feel.

But that reminded her she still had not seen her bed, and had no idea what sleeping accommodations they would come to.

When Adam came to rescue her at last, she saw that he too was looking exhausted, his lean face even more finely drawn than usual and his eyes red-rimmed. But he smiled at sight of her and said cheerfully, "Well, and how did you like your first day of army life?"

But she had already decided to put him straight at once. "Very well," she responded coolly. "But in future I prefer to ride with the regiment. Mrs. Delafield informs me a number of wives do, and it seems far preferable to being banished to the rear amid the dust. I promise I won't be a burden to either you or Hanson."

He looked astonished, and mildly amused, but after a moment made no protest. "Very well. You may have one of my mounts, and I daresay a saddle can be found for you. But are you sure? If you think you are tired now, think what it will be like after a day spent in the saddle, especially when you're not used to it. Your bones may ache now, but you'll ache in quite a different place, I promise you."

She shrugged. "Then I shall become used to it."

He made no more protest. She suspected he thought she would soon tire of her bargain, but he merely said teasingly, as they approached his tent, "You are now about to have your first taste of sleeping in a tent. It should be a new experience for you as well."

"At the moment I feel I could lay down on the ground right here and sleep for two days," she told him frankly. "A tent sounds like an unnecessary luxury. What time do we start tomorrow?"

"At first light, I'm afraid. Just when you're dropping into your second slumbers. But such is the life of an army wife."

But in truth she found his tent cramped, but surprisingly comfortable. She strongly suspected his batman, Beam, had been ordered to exceptional duty to prepare it for her, for it was clean and neat and smelled faintly of soap. Two camp chairs had been set out in front, with a table set for dinner, and mouth-watering smells were emanating from the cook-fire in the rear.

Adam gave her time to clean up, though she had nothing clean to change into, and could only brush out her habit as best she could. He seated her ceremoniously. "Our wedding dinner," he said in amusement, offering her a glass of miraculously chilled wine. "A vast improvement on our wedding night, I confess, but still lacking in a certain elegance. But are you really all right? You looked exhausted earlier. I'm sorry I had to neglect you so shamefully today."

She raised her glass to his toast and sipped gratefully at the wine. "I was thinking the same thing of you, that you looked exhausted." She said bluntly, "And I refuse to become an added burden to you. You must leave me to my own devices and not worry. I shall be fine, I promise you."

He smiled. "We shall see," was all he said.

It was evident that pains had been taken over the meal that first night and Reggie praised everything highly, but the one skinny fowl that composed their main course was tough and plainly cooked. Adam, tired as he was, only picked at it, and the sight drove her to another silent resolution. Cooking happened to be one of her few accomplishments, and she was determined not to be just another burden. It might be excessive pride, and very likely would make no difference anyway, but he was to be made to see that women were not the frail, helpless creatures he thought them. Doubtless there would be many more ways she could find to make herself useful, as the days passed. She had never yet seen a household, even a portable one such as this, run only by males that could not use a woman's touch.

And in the event, despite her fears the hurdle of the first night was gotten over with very little embarrassment after all. She was so tired she could indeed have fallen asleep where she sat, and Adam, taking in her weary countenance and drooping eyes, soon sent her firmly to bed. She said her sleepy good nights and retired, and it was not until she lay in the narrow campbed that Beam had prepared for her that she realized that she had no idea where her husband was going to be sleeping that night.

Even on the thought she fell asleep, only to be roused next morning while it was still dark. For a moment she could not think where she was, or why there should be such a din seemingly outside her very window.

Then she came fully awake as memory flooded back. She was astonished to realize she must not have stirred once her head touched her pillow, but rose hurriedly and fumbled into her clothes by the fitful lantern light. By the sounds of it the entire camp had been awake for some while and she dreaded keeping Adam waiting.

When she emerged into the chill dawn air, it was to find him calmly consuming breakfast, as if he had all the time in the world.

He also greeted her as if he had been doing so every day of his life, and he rose to seat her. "Good morning! I hoped to let you sleep a little longer. Did you sleep well?"

His matter-of-fact air did much to lessen her embarrassment in their absurd situation. "Not long, but oh, so well," she said truthfully. "I don't think I stirred all night. But where—" Then she stopped, annoyed with herself for asking.

But he answered cheerfully, "Where did I sleep? It was so nice a night, that I dossed down outside."

She bit her lip, but made herself go on. "In any event, I certainly did not mean to drive you from your own tent. Surely there is somewhere else—or even room enough for both of us if it comes to that?"

"No." He said it quite gently, but with a finality in his voice that had her blushing absurdly.

Then he rose and stretched himself, as if he had not just issued a decided rebuff. "What will you have to eat? There are eggs, but no bacon. I can't offer you much in the way of breakfast, I'm afraid."

She was still blushing hotly and was grateful for the darkness that hid her embarrassment. "Just some of that heavenly smelling coffee and a slice of bread will do me." Her instincts warned her to leave it alone, but she would not drive him from his own bed when she knew he would be liable to need all his rest. "That is all very well," she went on doggedly, "but your prejudices against women in the tail of the army begin to be understandable if you are determined to be so stupidly stubborn. What if it rains? You can hardly sleep out then."

He laughed at that. "You'd be surprised. In fact, I hope you won't be, for there are too many nights, when we are separated from our baggage, that you will find even the primitive comforts of a tent an unalloyed blessing. And I never know when I shall be sent ahead on some mission or another. Don't bother your head about that. But speaking of which, I have been busy this morning. My spare mare could carry you comfortably, for she's a silken mouth and is very well mannered. And I've had a saddle of mine converted— that is, if you are still of the same mind? I own I'd not like to be cooped up in a carriage all day, but I'm warning you a march is a very different thing from a gentle canter in the park. You are apt to rue your decision long before the day is over."

She unwillingly admitted defeat and finished her breakfast. It seemed that whatever their lopsided bargain, she was to have no right to worry about him.

The mare he produced proved to be a spirited-looking bay named Bella, whom she fell in love with at first sight. "Oh, but how can you bear to part with her?" she cried, stroking and making over her. "Besides, Mrs. Delafield warned me that an officer's remounts can be of crucial importance to him."

"Don't worry. She's scarcely up to my weight. I won her on a wager, as a matter of fact, and she's by no means trained to battle yet. I should have sold her, but you're right, she's a beauty, and so I couldn't bear to part with her. And now I'm glad I didn't, for she should be just the thing for you."

He tossed her into the saddle himself, but then regretfully had to take leave of her. He had his duties to attend to, and was already late.

"My dear sir," she said calmly, having by then got herself well in hand. "I shall do perfectly well on my own. Don't let me keep you."

"Adam," he corrected, busy adjusting her stirrup for her.

She smiled down at him suddenly. "Adam. You're right.

If we are to keep up this absurd bargain of ours, we must neither of us behave as if anything had changed between us. Now go and see to your men."

He stared up at her for a moment, almost as if dazzled, and she had the satisfaction of seeing him for once thrown out of his usual easy command of any situation. Then abruptly he did so, leaving her to the escort of the stolid Hanson, mounted on an ugly trooper.

As a companion the groom left a great deal to be desired, but she quickly discovered it was indeed better out in the open, and found herself enjoying at least the first part of the day. The bay mare was a pleasure to ride, and having left the vast flat Tierra de Campos behind, the scenery was interesting.

She knew little of where they were going, or what their ultimate purpose might be. They saw nothing of the French army, reportedly in full retreat before them, but now and then, from a long distance, could be caught the dull boom of artillery fire, so that it was clear some at least of the army were in contact with the French.

It was a sobering reminder. Several times she caught glimpses of men she knew, who waved to her or rode briefly up to speak to her. And once Adam came riding back down the line, an anxious expression on his face until he caught sight of her.

"How are you doing?" he demanded, searching her face for signs of fatigue.

"Oh, wonderfully. Very much better than yesterday, I can tell you," she answered cheerfully.

His expression lightened somewhat. "That's my girl," he said briefly, already turning away. "The devil's in it, I can't stay. I must go on ahead to reconnoiter. But Hanson will look after you."

She would have given much to be able to convince him she had no intention of becoming merely an added burden, when it was clear he had more than enough to worry him already. But he was already gone, and she did not see him for the rest of the day, until they called a halt at last, in the valley of the upper Ebro.

She was admittedly tired, and ached in some unaccustomed spots after her long day in the saddle, but she began to think optimistically that the difficulties of the march had been exaggerated. In fact, they had even passed through some villages, earlier in the day, where pretty girls had run out to offer the soldiers fruit and drinks, and tossed flowers at them.

But she discovered, when she dismounted, that she was so weary that her legs would not hold her. Had not Hanson been there, with his strong arm to catch her, she feared she might have fallen ignominiously.

Chapter 21

BUT WHEN ADAM returned, at dusk, dusty and sweat-streaked, he found her sitting before a pleasant meal, as calmly as if she had been bred to the life.

He looked a little startled, but promised to join her in five minutes. "For I've had nothing to eat all day, and I'm ravenous. But I begin to think I've again underestimated you, my dear. You look as fresh as a nosegay."

He was as good as his word, returning refurbished and freshly washed, his hair still damp. "Which reminds me," he said, forking into his meal and hungrily chewing. "I must get you a maid. She will doubtless be rough, but there should be someone among the camp followers with some training as a lady's maid."

"My dear sir, do you imagine I cannot exist without a maid?" she demanded in the liveliest astonishment.

"No, but she will lend you protection and respectability. And there will be times when I shall need Hanson and he can't stay beside you. Good Lord, what is this I'm eating?" he demanded, as if suddenly realizing.

"Do you like it?" she inquired somewhat anxiously.

"Like it? I thought for a moment I must have died and gone to heaven! This is your doing, I make no doubt, for Beam never produced a meal like this. But, my dear, you are not to be cooking for me, especially after a hard day in the saddle."

"You tend to your duties, Colonel Canfield, and I shall

tend to mine," she said sedately, well pleased by the results of her labors.

And certainly, as the days passed, she found many little ways to make herself useful. It did not take her long to discover Adam's batman, a quiet reserved individual, was no hand with a needle, for most of Adam's clothes and all of his socks were woefully worn. She managed to beg a needle and wool and busied herself in her spare moments with mending his shirts and socks, and sewing on buttons. Most of his wardrobe was incredibly shabby, as she had already learned all the other officers' were as well, for there was little ready money between them, and salaries had been in arrears for months. But then compared with her own wardrobe, which consisted of two dresses, one of them borrowed, he was the height of sartorial elegance.

News of her culinary skills soon spread. His friends grew in the habit of dropping by just at dinnertime, hoping to be invited to dine, and though Adam frequently protested, his words fell on deaf ears. It was the least she could do in their lopsided bargain.

And though it was a hard life, and she inevitably was exhausted by the end of a long day in the saddle, there was a rough pleasure in it. She began to see why Adam and his friends all liked it, for all their grumbling, and what had drawn Filipe to abandon his studies and the luxury of the life he was used to to go and fight in the mountains.

Once it began to rain heavily in the middle of the day, and Reggie soon found herself soaked to the skin. But since it was a warm rain, it scarcely seemed to matter, and there was no hope of getting out of it. The troopers beside her were soon trudging in mud up to their ankles, dragging their heavy guns, and compared to them she knew herself to have few complaints.

Then she looked up under the brim of her dripping hat to see Adam splashing his way toward her. He took in her drowned rat state and said angrily, "Hanson should have insisted you go back to ride with Mrs. Delafield! Have neither of you any sense? You will catch your death in this downpour."

She laughed at him through the rain dripping off her nose. "Oh, pooh! Do *you* catch pneumonia every time you get a wetting? Then neither will I. I am very well, I assure you. Go back to your duty."

He looked frustrated, but clearly had no time to stay arguing with her. After an impotent moment he shrugged and splashed away again.

And if the truth be known, she knew he was at considerably more risk of damaging his health than she was. She had already seen that he never spared himself, and frequently rode twice as many miles as anyone else, scouting out the terrain. She feared in that sense her presence did make more work for him, for she suspected he came back to check on her when he could scarce spare the time or energy.

But it was the only thing she regretted about this strange new life of hers. She had wholly failed to make Adam understand that far from being some hothouse flower that must be protected against every chill wind, she had never enjoyed herself more, despite the hardships.

Adam's friends thankfully seemed to accept her presence far more readily than he did himself, and for the most part paid her the supreme compliment of reverting to their normal behavior in her presence. They laughed and joked with her, paid her outrageous compliments, and soon stopped guarding their tongues or their manners around her. Captain Prescott, one of her most frequent visitors, eyed her in amusement one evening as she was stirring one of her concoctions over the fire, her ringlets damp with sweat and her face shiny, and said, "By God, Reggie, Adam doesn't deserve his fortune. You're a capital campaigner!"

They were waiting for Adam to return from one of his endless scouting expeditions. She feared he was working himself to the bone, but knew of no way of stopping him. She laughed and finished her stirring, then dropped into a camp chair set outside in the dusk. "Thank you. I only wish Adam agreed with you."

She lived in dread of the day, in fact, that he would pronounce that the way was safe for her to be dispatched to the rear. Or—even worse—that she would in the end prove unequal to the march, and have to fall out.

But that at least she was determined not to do. And she had been surprised at how quickly her body had adjusted to the demands placed upon it. It was a life she would have shuddered at only a few months ago, but now there was an odd satisfaction in such a physical existence. She slept dreamlessly every night, rose at dawn, and spent the better part of the day in the saddle, most of the time among rough troopers and none but the untalkative Joe Hanson for company. But for all that she had never been bored or restless, as she had frequently been in the overformal existence she had left behind. In fact that life might have belonged to someone else. For the moment there were only the demands of the march and the necessity to prove herself.

Adam had indeed found her a rough maid, named Betty, who willingly fetched and carried for her, but she returned every night to her husband, an infantryman, unless needed, and in any event was scarcely a companion.

But it was a far from lonely life. Over and over again Reggie could only marvel at the lightheartedness she found among Adam's friends. It seemed to her that after a tiring day in the saddle, and with any number more facing them, with at the end the possibility of a bloody battle, they should all have been seeking their beds. But she was soon to learn that the young officers, so charming and seemingly without cares, had the energy and stamina of mules. They thought nothing of a forty-mile march in sweltering heat, and were as apt to ride another ten miles to some dance or other, or get up an impromptu party, as to complain of fatigue.

They all were loud in their admiration of the meals she managed to produce out of the most meager of ingredients.

She was to find that the commissariat was always late, or failed to show at all, and learned early to dispatch Hanson to snare what likely-looking game they passed, or scrawny hen.

They had still seen no sign of the French army. At one point a rifle battalion had overtaken the baggage train in the rear of a French brigade and enjoyed a pretty little skirmish. But the French, apparently uncertain how much of the British army might be behind it, had soon taken to their heels, leaving all their baggage and accoutrements behind them. The riflemen had been in high fettle with their spoils, until Lord Wellington had ordered the French baggage to be sold by auction.

But if this incident struck a certain chill in her at the unwelcome reminder of their ultimate purpose, the only emotion she could read in Adam's friends—or indeed in any of the soldiers—was a lifting of the spirits at the idea they might be coming in contact with the main French army at last.

But that evening, they were merely lamenting the usual dilatoriness of the commissariat. "In fact, without you, my dear Reggie, we should all be dining on acorns," asserted Captain Prescott with his slow grin. "Doubtless you noticed we are all on short rations again tonight."

Another officer who had dropped by after dinner to enjoy a smoke groaned. "Don't remind me. I personally dined on badly tainted beef and hard bread. My men are reduced to frying pork strips on their bayonets over the fire. By the time that da—I mean, that dashed canteen shows up, we shall be in France, no doubt."

"Where the devil did your men get pork?" demanded young Lord George indignantly. "*Mine* were grumbling by their fires and nursing their empty bellies, poor brutes."

"Well, if they've not enough ingenuity to liberate a lost pig now and then, I've no sympathy with them," retorted the first.

"Aye, and if Wellington comes to hear of if, you'll find

yourself explaining their ingenuity to his lordship!" said Captain Prescott in amusement. "I admit we are in a cleft stick. If the canteen is late or missing, as it is half the time, and our men feed on the country, his lordship is irate and is apt to have you up before him. But if they fall out of the march due to hunger, or God forbid, are not up to fighting strength, you're even more certain to hear about that. We can't win."

"The trick is to just take care to be discreet. I dined like a king off a stolen hen, but you don't hear me boast of it," put in Captain Colville rather smugly.

"No, and we didn't hear you inviting any of us to dinner, either!" complained Lord George. "At least Reggie takes pity on our suffering now and then. But of far more importance to me than the lost canteen, which is only what I expect, is where we are going. Are we really going to come to grips with the Frogs sometime soon, or did I dream it?"

"Ask Adam," put in someone else lazily, sitting on a turned-up kettle. "He's always the first to know the news."

Adam had just come in, late as usual, and now wearily joined then. "In this case, I'm as much in the dark as the rest of you," he confessed. "But I wouldn't be surprised— and soon, unless I miss my guess."

The others sat up. "If I thought you meant it—!" exclaimed Lord George. "But ten to one it's all a hum, and we'll be back to chasing our tails again. As for catching up with the main body of the French army, I'm beginning to think it don't exist."

Adam grinned, but there was a certain grimness behind his eyes. In the time Reggie had been with the army he had lost a touch of his famed insouciance, and was looking decidedly drawn and strained. "It exists all right, and old Hookey means to catch up with it, or kill us all in the attempt. I've been over the ground for the next few days' march—that's where I've been all day, while your lot lounged at ease in the saddle—and I promise you no one but his lordship would believe we could get troops over such country."

He spared a quick glance at Reggie, pleasantly tired and comfortable before the fire. In truth she was scarcely listening. She was content to sit, chin on her hand, for once her everpresent mending forgotten in her lap, and only half awake. She ached in every bone, but there was something very comforting about their lighthearted chatter, in English, and the knowledge that she was among her own again, after so many years. She found she cared very little at the moment where they were going tomorrow, or what danger the future might hold. She was comfortable and oddly happy.

As usual the men had largely forgotten she was present, but far from feeling slighted, she was grateful for it. She far preferred to listen to their talk, unrestrained by having to do the civil to her. She thought sleepily that that would have been one of the things she would have most regretted her presence changing. That Adam could not enjoy the company of his friends without fear of offending or excluding her, or them feeling the need to alter their language or conversation because of her, would be unforgivable.

It was Adam who unexpectedly put a stop to the pleasant evening. He rose and threw the butt of his cigar into the fire with a repressed violence and said abruptly, "It is more than time you were in bed, my dear. You are three parts asleep already."

She glanced up, startled out of her pleasant fuddle. But she was indeed almost asleep, and so rose and bid them all a pleasant good night. She did not see the amused glances cast by his friends, as they too rose and discreetly made their good nights.

Or know that Adam strode up and down outside the tent for a long time, long after she was almost instantly asleep and dreaming, cursing himself for his folly. He was wishing, with a vehemence that would undoubtedly have disturbed her sleep if she had known of it, that he had her safe in England. For she was not the only one to worry about what would happen if she were ever forced to fall out of the march; and he knew better than anyone that during the next few days she would be put very much to the test.

Chapter 22

THEY WERE UP at dawn as usual the next morning. The incredibly high peaks of the Cantabrian mountains had been looming over them for days, and Reggie soon saw that Adam had been right. It seemed they were to cross terrain she would not have guessed suitable for anything but a mountain goat, let alone an army.

Adam had continued to look grim that morning over breakfast, and had completely lost the lighthearted charm she had so much loved. He said little, but stared at her hard as he tossed her into the saddle, though he was the one who looked as if he had not had any sleep. She guessed he was fearing she would never be able to make the climb, and the knowledge merely stiffened her spine and made her smile down at him with more than her usual cheerfulness.

He blinked, but after a brief moment merely turned away.

And for the first part of the march she found herself not much more hard-pressed than usual. For days they had moved through luxurious valleys intersprinkled with picturesque hamlets, vineyards, and flower gardens, which all had been a far cry from the hot and dusty plains they had left behind. As for the foothills they were now traveling through, they were easy enough to traverse. It was only the stark peaks that loomed above them that made her a little giddy.

Certainly when they started to climb she began to see why Adam had appeared worried. That first day they struggled up paths she would not have dreamed passable, but her own plight was nothing to the foot soldiers', who had to trudge every step of the way on foot and haul their guns up after them. By the end of the day she was breathless with fatigue and so weary she did not stop to eat any dinner, grateful for once that his duty kept Adam elsewhere. She dropped onto her cot and went to sleep immediately, not to move until the camp began to stir at dawn the next morning.

The next day was even worse. Adam, who had covered the ground at least once already, was everywhere. His eyes were gritty with fatigue, but whenever she glanced up he seemed to be there. She would smile tiredly at him, almost too exhausted to speak, and his expression would lighten, if only for the moment. "I'm fine," she would manage. "Don't worry about me."

Even she knew by then it was a futile request. That second day she saw grown men fall by the wayside, to turn black in the face and die horribly. She averted her eyes from such sights, sick and dizzy herself with fatigue and heat and the altitude. And she often suspected it was only her determination to prove Adam wrong that enabled her to go on.

By the fourth day the way was so steep she had to dismount and walk herself, up grades that frequently had her knees as high as her head. Hanson, plainly worried, stayed close beside her, and Adam was often there, though his worried expression had come to annoy her, as if he were only waiting for her to fail. Whenever she would see him she would straighten and try to hide her exhaustion, though it was impossible to still her harsh panting or disguise the sweat soaking her face and body. But to his anxious inquiries she would only return with what little breath she could muster that she was all right, he was not to worry about her.

That day his expression did not even lighten at the reassurance. The number of men and even horses and mules forced to drop out had grown so great that she no longer even noticed the dead carcasses along the way, unless they became an obstacle in her path. Sometimes the way was so narrow and the drop so steep that exhausted men missed their step and fell, screaming, to land horribly on the rocks below; and once a horse and the gun it was dragging slipped to fall, bumping and echoing sickeningly until both reached the bottom.

But by then Reggie had no energy left to spare for such horrors. It required all her concentration to keep one foot in front of another. Her breath was coming in short painful gasps, and her head reeled as if she had a fever. Hanson, beside her, did what he could, but he was in dire straits himself, as were most of those around her.

Whenever they stopped, which was frequently, to allow those ahead to make their slow painful way, she hung on to the bridle and leaned her weary body against the mare, fearful that if she ever sat down she would not get back up again. It had gone far beyond her mere dread of being forced to fall to the rear and be left behind. Now she dreaded every minute to fall by the wayside and die, with blackened face and a horrible froth on her lips as so many were doing around her.

It kept her upright when she did not think she could go on any longer. She was only thankful that Adam had been sent on ahead, and thus was not there to see if she did fail.

Time lost all meaning to her. There ceased being a past and future, for there seemed to be nothing beyond the necessity to take another step, to drag herself up again and yet again, to ignore the roaring in her ears and the pounding in her temples, and the gasping painful breaths that rasped her throat and made it still drier. Hanson was laboring beside her, and even the horses showed great patches of sweat and were trembling in every limb. She wondered bleakly what she would do if the mare fell, for then she knew she could not go on. But it did no good to think of that. Every thought must be concentrated on taking the next step and then the next.

One foot. Another. The reins were so slippery in her hands she could scarcely hold them, and black stars danced before her vision. She shut her eyes to try to block them out, and discovered she was reeling, no longer certain which way was up or down. The ground was tilting strangely, and she was floating. It was a relief to give herself up to that floating sensation, but there was a strange harsh gasping in her ears that disturbed her. It annoyed her and she wished it would go away, until she realized it was her own painful gasps that she was hearing.

That shocked her, and she opened her eyes again, but nothing seemed real about her, and the colors were all wrong. Everything was curiously foreshortened, too, seeming flat and without depth or substance, like a picture badly painted. Hanson, beside her, said something, but no sound reached her. She tried to reassure him, for she knew he was worried, and he had no need. She felt fine now. More than fine. She could march on forever in this floating state, feeling nothing and pleasantly removed from the struggle of all the others around her.

Then she was lying against something warm and vital, though she could not remember having fallen, and someone was saying urgently, "Open your mouth, darling. Drink this. Come on, open your mouth!"

She opened it to say incredulously, "Adam—?" Then something fiery passed between her lips and burned her throat, jerking her completely awake, coughing and choking.

"That's my girl," his voice said, sounding strained even to her ears. "Here, just a little more. You'll soon be all right."

She managed to say indignantly, "Of course I will."

Another voice she recognized as belonging to Captain Prescott said in relief, "She'll be all right, Adam. You should have known she was equal to anything."

She opened her eyes, absurdly pleased by the compliment, to find herself lying on the dusty ground, her head and shoulders held closely in Adam's arms, and his face very close to her own. He looked haggard, his eyes sunken with fatigue, and for a moment she scarcely recognized him. Then she realized that his face was dark with dust and sweat.

Something seemed to snap in him as he realized she was all right. "Sweet Christ!" he said in a voice she scarcely recognized. "This is what I've reduced her to. Doesn't anyone understand? Whether or not by some miracle she doesn't fall out this time, this is no life for a woman! I should have insisted upon sending her back, and by God I will the first opportunity I get. Worse, I can't do my duty properly for worrying about her. It's a damnable situation in every way, I tell you!"

She stirred, realizing her worst nightmares were coming true. "No, no—I can make it," she croaked. "Only don't make me fall out! I beg of you—"

She thought he choked, but he said only, after a moment, "My dear! Does it mean so much to you?"

She was beyond pride. "Yes, yes! I was overcome by the heat, but I'm better now. You'll see I can go on. You needn't worry about me. Hanson can take care of me. Only please, please don't leave me behind!"

He said something under his breath, then took her hands gently in his and held them tightly. "My darling, we're through. You've somehow made it while far stronger men were dropping like flies. The worst is over now. You've made it. We've stopped for the night, and tomorrow will be much easier, I promise you."

She strained to see the truth in his eyes, and then relaxed with a little glow of satisfaction. "Good," she murmured. "I told you I could keep up."

She remembered little more of that evening. The baggage train had been wholly unable to keep up with the climb, and so as usual there was no food for the exhausted troops, most of whom were too spent to care, and no tents. Reggie remembered Adam rolling her up in a blanket, as if she had been a child, and as soon as she lay down beside the fire she went out like a light.

She woke, wonderfully refreshed and hungry, to find her cheek pillowed on a rough, warm surface, and aware of being blissfully warm. It took her a moment to realize the rough surface was the wool of Adam's jacket, and the heavenly warmth was the result of being held tightly in his arms.

She lifted her head to watch him, wanting nothing but to prolong that magical moment. He slept with the concentration of total exhaustion, his face looking somehow strange but dearly familiar in that unguarded moment. He needed a shave, and he looked very vulnerable, as he had more than a year ago when she had first rescued him; and not the tough, distracted soldier with the worried frown between his brows that she had grown accustomed to seeing in the last weeks.

It struck her then that she had done that to him, and she could have wept with sadness and regret. He had been right after all. Worry for her had changed and aged him from the carefree soldier she had once known. It had been wrong of her to thrust herself upon him, to selfishly wish to stay for her own sake, when it only made his own task ten times more difficult. Even the horror and exhaustion of yesterday's march had already faded, and she knew she would willingly have endured a thousand such rather than be banished to safety and inactivity once more. But perhaps it was not fair to him, torn as he was between responsibility for her and his duty, as he had once described seeing others before him.

And she realized as well in that moment that she would not for anything be responsible for making him less than he was, whatever the cost to herself. That was not love as she understood it, and she had loved him for a very long time now. There could be no longer any doubt.

Then he stirred and opened sleep-blurred eyes and looked straight at her. For a moment his face softened and he smiled spontaneously and she would have sworn there was pleasure in his face at sight of her. She knew it was a moment that might have to last her a very long time. A very long time indeed.

But it lasted briefly enough. Almost as quickly full consciousness returned to his face, and he stiffened, as if becoming aware of his arms tightly around her. He rubbed his eyes and mumbled, "I'm sorry. I must have fallen asleep. I meant to stay awake and keep the fire going. Were you cold?"

She was blushing by now, but said merely, "No, gloriously warm. And don't apologize. I was immensely grateful for your shoulder."

He seemed to have recovered himself by then and retreated into his usual pleasant mask where she was concerned. "But nevertheless it is scarcely part of our—agreement," he pointed out dryly, and he rose abruptly. "How do you feel? You were about all in yesterday."

She rose, too, telling herself she was a fool to regret the waking of the camp all about them and the necessity to get ready for the day's march. He was right. That was not in their agreement, and in light of her new discovery, she dared not forget that for a moment.

Also true to Adam's word, the worst was indeed over. That day's march bore no relation to the previous one. There were admittedly times, picking her way down the precarious trail, or forced to dismount on some almost perpendicular stretch, when she wondered if going downhill were not almost as bad as going up. But if nothing else it required far less energy.

Predictably, the soldier's spirits rose as they descended the other side of the mountains they had so painfully climbed, and the survivors soon even began to boast of the ordeal. She heard a number of them admitting they had never endured a worse march, or seen more troops falling out in all their years in the Peninsula. Trust old Hooknose to take them by the worst route, and then wonder why it took them so long to get there!

Reggie was aware of a momentary pride that she had made the march with them and not fallen out; until she remembered it was all too likely to be her last. But such gloomy thoughts could not long survive, for rumor came back during the long day that the First and Light Divisions, heading the struggling British columns, had debouched so rapidly from the passes they had overtaken a column of the retreating French, under Reille, who had believed the British far behind and had considered the mountain roads wholly impassable. After a short, sharp engagement, the French had retreated in confusion and a few hundred prisoners had been taken.

At once the entire army quickened its steps, exhausted and foot-weary soldiers suddenly erect and eager, their weariness and even their hungry bellies forgotten. All were anxious to encounter the enemy, and the grueling five-day march over ground no one but Wellington would have thought practicable for an army was at once forgotten, since it enabled them to wholly confound the French. Everyone admitted that his lordship, as usual, knew what he was doing, despite the cursing his troops had accorded him during that forced and brutal march.

Reggie's heart was not quite so eager, but she had no intention of revealing the fact. When they at last emerged from the mountains to end up on the plain before Vittoria, where the French army was encamped, her pulse accelerated as well at the ragged cheer raised by the exhausted troops. They had come up with the enemy at long last.

Chapter 23

ADAM'S FRIENDS were in high fettle that night. Half a dozen of them came by after supper, laughing and joking, as if no battle loomed tomorrow. Indeed, Reggie could only conclude that their good spirits arose from the promise of coming to grips with the enemy at last.

She had to make an effort to put on a good face before Adam's friends. She could not help wondering how many of them might be dead by tomorrow night, and discovered that her enjoyment of her new life had its price. Death was so familiar to all of them that they took it for granted, and if any of them were afraid, they hid it well behind their laughing, sun-bronzed faces. But it was all new to her and she knew a terrible fear that gripped at the pit of her stomach and made it impossible for her to eat.

She also knew instinctively that she could communicate none of her fear to anyone else. To clutch at hands at parting or utter sentimental rubbish would do nothing but upset everyone. And so, when the time came, they took their leave cheerfully, with a laugh or a jest, and faded into the warm darkness, perhaps never to be seen alive again.

It was a morbid idea she did her best to banish from her thoughts, for Adam would appreciate even less than his friends her waxing sentimental over their parting. Certainly he should never guess how little she slept that night, or what dark thoughts haunted her.

And in the event the parting from Adam, when it came the next morning, was absurdly anticlimactic. Reggie had risen long before daylight to discover Adam already up before her, standing while he gulped down a cup of strong coffee and issued last-minute orders to his groom.

He looked handsome and as normal as if it were any other morning. But he said abruptly as soon as he saw her, "I was hoping you would sleep longer. Hanson has his orders. He is to keep you well to the rear, out of danger, and you are to obey him. I want your promise on that."

She wanted to clutch at him, beg him not to go, cling to him for the last minutes left to them. But of course she did none of that. Instead, she rather blindly accepted the cup of coffee he poured for her and said quietly, "Yes, of course. Don't worry about me."

He finished his own coffee with a gulp. "That's my girl! I must go."

He hesitated, and then added offhandedly, "He has his instructions as well, if anything should happen to me. Not that anything will. You must know by now I bear a charmed life. But he will see you safely back to England, and my family will look after you there. Prescott, too, has promised to look after you, so you have nothing to worry about."

Her smile was infinitely sad, and she wondered at the blindness of men. Her own future was the last thing on her mind at the moment. But all she said again was, "Yes. Don't think of it."

He shrugged, as if glad to have the unpleasant duty over, and finished buttoning the tight red jacket that became him so well. He had meant to be a comfort, she knew. He could not know what a cold ache his light words had struck in her soul, or that it was all she could do to keep her face as light and unemotional as his own through her growing terror.

It was a control she would have reason to be immensely grateful for later. At the moment she could not prevent herself adding, in a tight little voice that strained to remain normal and she feared scarcely succeeded, "You will—be careful won't you?"

"Oh, Lord yes." He was annoyingly careless. "Don't forget, I have been through a dozen such engagements with scarcely more than a scratch. And I confess I will be glad to get this campaign over. Frankly it has been damnable."

It was a strike to the heart. She did not need to ask why he had found this campaign more trying than the others.

Somewhat to her surprise, while she was still reeling from that, he unexpectedly caught her to him and gave her a brief hard kiss. Then he was gone.

It was only much later, when it was far too late, that she was to recall all the things she might have said to him, and all the things he would never know, and she wished she had said them whatever the cost. But at the moment, she had thought it just as well, if only for the sake of her pride. He had nothing but the battle on his mind, anyway, and did not need the burden of her own weight of fear and regret.

Nor did it help that all around her she could hear cheerful preparations for the coming battle. Soldiers were facing death, and seemed only glad they were having the chance to square up to Johnny Crapaud at last. She heard laughter and amused taunts, and more than one of the wiry, sunburnt troopers around her was whistling or humming a gay scrap of a tune as they primed their pieces and saw to their gunpowder.

It was only those to be left behind who showed grim faces, like the dour Hanson, and one or two stricken wives, whom she saw white with fear and near to fainting. It was pride as well that made Reggie assume a cheerful aspect when she bade farewell to one or two of her particular friends, for several, like Captain Prescott, stopped to exchange a cheery word with her.

For Adam's sake she kept up a brave front, wishing them luck calmly and trying not to imagine how many of them might not come back whole, or at all, by the end of the day. Only to Captain Prescott did she let a little of her anxiety show. He was on horseback and had stopped to speak to her briefly, for he had no time to dismount and talk.

She put an anxious hand on his stirrup and asked, "You will be careful, won't you?"

Like Adam, he answered cheerfully, "Oh, Lord yes!" Then he must have seen something in her face, for she knew already how sharp-eyed he was, and he added, "Don't worry, my dear. Adam may be the devil of a reckless fool, but he does bear a charmed life. And I'll keep my eye out for him."

She said with difficulty, "Thank you. But you, too. I can't bear—I'm sorry. I should not burden you with my own fears. Adam would consider this proof a woman has no place in the army. But—take care!"

She was obliged to turn away from him quickly to hide her tears. He looked in concern after her, but had no time, and in the end was forced to spur his horse somewhat savagely away.

And then they were gone. The place seemed immensely quiet and forlorn once the last regiment had marched away. Hanson was waiting somewhat impatiently, her mare already saddled and their little tent struck, everything loaded on mules. Hanson had his orders, and meant to follow them to the letter.

He took her back to the baggage train, where she dismounted and tried not to think of what was happening up ahead. Captain Prescott had assured her cheerfully that the French were spread on too wide a front and had too few guards at the bridges, and would easily be beaten, but it was hard to believe such easy words, especially after the guns began. She shuddered at the first heavy booming, and soon the noise was so steady and unbearable that she longed to stop up her ears, only that she could still feel the vibrations even then.

She pictured the battlefield, as she had seen it that morning from the heights where they had been camped, and could not help envisioning the desperate fighting taking place there.

It was a misty morning, and even rained a little, but it

soon cleared up and developed into the usual hot June day. But despite the heat, Reggie found that she was shivering. Her skin was clammy, and she was both hot and cold, in turns. As she had envisioned, the waiting was unbearable. She was no longer in sight of the field, but the air above was soon thick with smoke, and the roar of the cannon and the sharper rattle of the muskets were unceasing.

Hanson remained stolidly by her side, though she tried to send him away. She feared Adam might need him, for she knew by then how desperately important an officer's remounts might be. But Hanson had his orders and turned a deaf ear to her urgings.

But far too soon the wounded began to make their way to the rear, and suddenly she found more than enough to occupy her. The nature of the wounds she saw was so horrible that it did nothing to alleviate her terror, but soon there was little time for anything but tending to the dead and dying men all around her.

She cleaned and dressed the more superficial of the wounds, brought water to an endless line of parched and sunburnt soldiers, and gave what comfort she could to the more seriously wounded and the dying. Far too many of the wounds were beyond her meager skill, and the surgeons were kept busy, sewing up great gaping wounds and sawing off shattered limbs.

She was far from missish, but at first the sight and smells had her gagging and feeling faint. But far too soon she became deadened to the sight of blood and the horrible stench, and even the nightmare screams of the wounded. Most lay bravely, however, with wounds that still made her stomach rise up and threaten to betray her, and frequently died as quietly, there in the hot sun.

Hanson tried once or twice to pull her away, saying in his rough way that the master would not approve, and she had no business being there. But she was deaf to his words. It was impossible to turn her back when so many were in need, and soon, thankfully, she was too weary and inundated with horror to have any energy left for her own private hell.

Even so, she dreaded each time she approached a wounded officer, fearing to find it was someone she knew, or even Adam himself. Each time she gave up a silent prayer when it turned out to be a stranger, his face gray and blackened with smoke from the guns, and his teeth clenched against unbearable pain.

They were all pitifully grateful to her for her few attentions, and clung to her hand or followed her progress with their eyes. More than once a soldier died in her arms, and whether it was a hardened trooper recruited from the worst slums of London, or a beardless boy, she could not help weeping.

Once, when she hurried to help a slight figure left leaning against a wagon wheel in the sun, one arm bloody and swathed in bandages, it was not the face of a stranger. Lord George Austerby, of the ginger whiskers and brash manner, lay with his eyes closed, his face so altered she scarcely recognized him for a moment.

He looked up when she knelt down beside him and held a cup of water to his lips. He drank thirstily, and only then seemed to recognize her, for he summoned up the ghost of his old grin. "Reggie? Shouldn't be here—Adam wouldn't approve—" he managed.

He glanced down at his bloodstained bandages and added awkwardly, with a heart-tearing twist to his lips, "Not so lucky this time. But what a battle. Best ever." He closed his eyes weakly again, his fragile strength clearly spent.

Reggie had already seen the bandaged right arm that stopped horribly short. Pity and grief almost overwhelmed her, but that would do him no good. Instead she looked around frantically for a surgeon, fearing he was dying, so gray his face and sunken his eyes, despite the ghost of his gay little smile.

But even as she started up, his good hand gripped her

and he opened his eyes again, saying abruptly, "Don't go. Must tell you—"

There he stopped again, as if gathering strength, and she knew a buzzing in her ears and a rising horror, knowing somehow already what he was going to say. "Adam—?" she managed.

He shook his head faintly, having room to feel sorry for her in his own tragedy. "Dead. Saw him fall. Sorry. But thought . . . better hear from me . . . Dev'lish good fellow, Adam . . ."

His eyes closed again then, and Reggie rose almost automatically and called one of the busy surgeons to him. He took a hurried look and said gruffly, "Little I can do for him. He'll either live or he won't. See if you can have him carried out of the sun, at least." Then he took a look at her face and added more kindly, "Friend of yours?"

She hardly knew what she replied. She felt a curious distance from all of it. The news that Adam was dead would no doubt overwhelm her later, but now there were too many living who needed her help to have time to grieve over the dead. She saw Lord George carried to a place under the trees, providing a little pitiful shade in the flaring heat, and bent over the next one, doing what needed to be done in a dream.

It was over. Over. Over. None of it seemed real and Adam was dead. She bandaged wounds, gave water, and listened to the dying confessions and appeals almost woodenly, feeling blessedly numb. Tomorrow—next week—next year and all the years for the rest of her life she would have time to feel the gaping pain of his absence. But now there was necessary work to be done.

By the time the hot sun began to fall she was covered in dust and sweat, her hair fallen untidily down her back and her habit covered in bloodstains. She scarcely noticed. She was not even aware when the constant booming of the cannon began to lessen, and the sharp counterpoint of the musket fire grew more widely spaced.

Then someone grabbed her arm and a voice said her name, sharply. She turned, thinking it merely someone else needing her help.

For a dozen pounding heartbeats she was incapable of accepting the truth her eyes told her. For his part Adam took in her extreme pallor, and said almost angrily, "Reggie! What the devil are you doing? And where in perdition has Hanson got to? I leave you in his care, only to return to find you exhausted and scarcely able to stand."

She looked at him as if in a dream. The smart uniform she had so admired at the ball in Madrid, so long ago, was scarcely recognizable, and there was an ugly wound in his left thigh, covered by a dirty and stained bandage. His face was blackened almost beyond recognition, and his voice was but a hoarse echo of his usual tones. But he was alive. Miraculously alive.

She put out one hand, half afraid to touch him for fear he would melt away under her eyes. The roaring in her ears had become a torrent, and her long-forgotten stomach was in imminent danger of rebelling. "Adam—" she managed in a croak.

Then when he frowned and tightened his hold on her arm, she broke abruptly away and fled as if for her life.

Chapter 24

ADAM LIMPED after her. "Reggie! What the——? Damn it, hold up, I can't go so fast."

She didn't pause. She was afraid she would be ignominiously sick in front of him, and knew that in her present state she would never be able to hide her feelings from him.

Gratefully she reached the tent and ducked inside, leaning against a chest and panting, willing herself not to throw up or faint. Her head was whirling and she felt hot and cold all over, and as if she were encased in a deadening fog.

But despite his wounded leg, Adam proved to be surprisingly close behind her. The next moment she heard him swear as he jarred his leg, then he came in rapidly after her, saying in a voice of concern, "Reggie—my dear—what—?"

That almost defeated her. She said drearily, as if repeating a lesson, "They told me you were dead. They told me you were dead."

There was a moment's silence. Then he said helplessly, "Oh, my dear. In that case I'm sorry I startled you so."

Suddenly she straightened, amazingly, gloriously angry. "Startled me? *Startled me?* Oh, dear God! The things I've seen today . . . and then you . . . and all the time . . ." she blinked back the hot, futile tears, beyond caring what she revealed to him, "And all the time you—*you* were out there enjoying yourself immensely, I have no doubt!"

He actually laughed. "Not all the time, no. But darling, just listen!"

That did it. She began to move around wildly, dragging

out what few possessions she owned. "Well, if you needed your proof, you have it! You win! I'm not suited to such a life. I am exactly the sort of weak woman you despise, cluttering up the army and interfering with your work. You can hustle me off to Madrid or London or Timbuktu, for all I care, and enjoy your little war in peace."

"Darling, darling, you little fool!" he said, limping around in front of her and forcibly taking the hairbrush she was holding away from her. "I know you are upset, but what nonsense is this?"

"Don't you think I know you have been waiting for me to fail? You admitted from the beginning that women didn't belong in the t-tail of the army, and were only waiting the opportunity to s-send me away. Well, now you can do so with a clear conscience. You're right. I couldn't stand another day like t-today."

Instead of betraying any triumph, to her surprise he began to complete the havoc she had already caused by searching through her scattered belongings. "Where the devil has Hanson put the brandy?" he demanded wrathfully. "You clearly need a drink, for you're not making any sense. And I confess I could use one as well."

That at least gave her pause. She looked again at his exhausted face and the stiff leg he was so clearly trying not to call attention to, and said, stricken, "Oh, God—! I sent Hanson to fetch what brandy and wine he could to give to the wounded. I'm sorry. I never thought—"

He grinned and said with appalling cheerfulness, "Well, if you thought I was dead, I agree it little mattered. But since I am very much alive, and you are clearly on the edge of hysterics, it seems we could both do with some."

That stung. "I'm not on the edge of hysterics!" she insisted wildly.

He smiled at her with annoying amusement evident in his face and something else she dared not put a name to. "No? Otherwise you wouldn't be talking such rank nonsense. But since we are out of brandy, and some stimulus to the system is obviously called for, it seems we are reduced to this." And he pulled her roughly in his arms and began to kiss her.

She struggled with him for a moment, until he stiffened as if she had jarred his injured leg. That brought her to her senses. She said quite distinctly, "Damn you! Damn you!" and weakly began to cry.

He laughed and kissed her wet cheeks and then her wet lashes as she cried even harder. "Don't, my love," he said breathlessly. "If you only knew how little sleep I have had in the last weeks, knowing you were so near and yet not daring to do anything about it. And if you don't look up soon, so that I can kiss you again properly, I won't be responsible for my actions. Ah, that's better."

She had been betrayed into looking up, and instantly paid the penalty, for his kiss this time deprived her of all protest, and even breath.

The next moment he had drawn back, sounding more than breathless himself, and said ruefully, "So much for my intentions! We both need a change of clothes and a bath, and it is hardly the romantic setting I was determined to give you, but I have waited long enough for my wedding night, and I have discovered I can wait no longer. If you still have any wild and foolish notions of an annulment, my love, you'd better speak now, for in a moment I warn you it will be far too late."

"Adam—" When he looked at her, that same disturbing light in his eyes, she discovered she was not even sure herself what she had been going to say. It seemed she was beyond making any protests.

It seemed he was, too. He groaned and said in a voice she scarcely recognized as his, "And when you look at me like that, my darling, it is clear it is already too late." And then he kissed her again, with increasing roughness.

And if she had been dreaming of this moment ever since that time in Madrid, almost a year ago, or—if she was honest—even longer, she saw quickly that her dreams had after all been but pale lifeless things in face of reality. She had been longing for moonbeams, but there was no room any longer between them for such absurd fantasies. There was only the hunger of his kiss, as if he had been starved for a very long time, and the almost physical pain from the tightness of his arms about her.

Then he laughed—distinct triumph in the sound this time—and loosened his grip somewhat. "And now, sweetheart," he said, and laughed again, "and now it is more than time for both of us to rid ourselves of our filthy clothes."

If it occurred to her, belatedly and far too late, that this was but the overreaction of the end of battle, the inevitable letdown of fear and horror and relief, it was, as she had already known, far too late to save her. And she did not need to be told that this was an Adam she had never seen before. His passion drove everything before it, and she had neither the strength nor the will to save herself, or even him.

And if it was not the setting of her foolish dreams, in the hot tent with the last of the daylight still seeping in, and both of them tired and dirty and emotionally spent, she knew as well that her sanitized dreams had been but poor pitiful things that betrayed her complete ignorance of what could be between a man and a woman. When he swiftly undressed her she weakly let him, and when he even more hastily tried to strip off his own sweat-stained garments, she not only made no protest, but helped him protect his wounded leg against knocking.

He laughed at that and unconsciously echoed her own thoughts. "Not the romantic scene I had envisioned, I'm afraid. I didn't want to take you for the first time in a filthy camp, with too many people around and none of the romantic trappings like candlelight and champagne. But I find it doesn't matter. Nothing matters but this."

But for once she was scarcely even listening. "Adam, your poor leg!" she cried in horror.

"It's nothing. Don't! *Don't* my darling! God, come here. There is only so much I can bear, and we have long passed it. If you only knew what you have put me through. Oh, Reggie, my little love. My wife."

A long, long time later, when she could think again, Reggie remembered that oddly possessive cry, and all that followed. She said almost dreamily, held close in his warm arms and her head comfortably pillowed on his chest, "You never wanted to marry me. You made it clear from the beginning you wanted no commitments, and disliked women cluttering up the tail of the army."

He stirred lazily. "Hmm? If I did, you soon managed to change my mind. And as for women cluttering up the tail of the army, you must know that I have long since been forced to eat my words."

She roused at that indignantly. "You have not! You were still going to send me away at the first opportunity. You said so."

"For your own sake, you little fool, not mine. Don't you know that in a few short weeks you have made me so comfortable and worked yourself so much into my life that I have trouble envisioning how I ever lived without you? To have a home-cooked meal ready for me at the end of the day, my clothes mended, and my foolish little habits catered to—what man could resist? Or did you think it had escaped my notice that you have somehow discovered I detest overstrong tea, or too much chatter in the morning, or any other of the hundred and one things you see to without complaint? It is I who have been unworthy. Prescott says I don't deserve you, and he's right. If I wanted you to go away, it was purely for your safety, and not my own convenience. I was for once trying to do the decent thing. And anyway, you were the one who insisted our marriage was to be only a temporary one! I feared I had forced you into it against your will. Why else do you think I've managed to keep my hands off you all this time? To the detriment of my own health, I might add, and frequently my duty as well. So long as things remained as they were between us, I quickly discovered I needed to send you away for my own sanity."

"But all your prejudices against women in the army—?"

"Were just that," he said firmly. "Prejudices. You have proved yourself over and over again, my darling. Besides—"

She still could not believe him. "But your worry about me—it has added an extra burden, I know it has," she persisted. "It was the one thing I couldn't argue against in your determination to send me away."

"Then I will just have to get used to it. Anyway, I long since discovered I am fated to worry about you wherever you are. I suspect it will prove easier in the long run to keep you under my eye. Unless, of course, you persist in exhausting yourself as you did today in nursing every soldier in the army. Besides—"

She roused herself at that at long last, as if emerging from a wonderful dream. "The battle! Good God, how could I have forgotten it?"

He grinned wickedly. "You may have had other things on your mind."

But she was this time not to be distracted. "I haven't even asked how it went. What must you think of me?"

"If you want an answer to your first question any time soon, I think perhaps I had better not answer that one. Besides, I had prided myself that I had answered it fairly sufficiently already."

At her blush he relented. "But as a matter of fact, I have been trying to tell you for some time now. Even before we got—er—distracted." Suddenly she could see the blaze of excitement in him, and wondered how she could have missed it before. "We have won!" he told her. "The French are completely romped! When I left the field, King Joseph and his minions had abandoned it so fast they left behind almost everything. Our soldiers, curse 'em for the ragtag scoundrels they are, were busy looting what looked to be literally a king's ransom of money and stolen treasures, for rumor has it Joseph had a half million in sterling secreted among his personal effects, meant for the war effort, not to mention all the treasures he had stolen from Spain. I myself saw one cutthroat with a rolled up Velasquez in his possession." He grinned, no longer able to control his excitement. "His lordship will have a high old time getting them back into formation by tomorrow to follow up on our victory."

She was staring at him as if she could not quite take it in. As if aware of it, he said excitedly, "Don't you understand? The French had been driven completely out of Spain at last! It's over. We have won! I can scarcely believe it even yet myself, but it's true. It's too soon to tell yet, but I suspect Napoleon is on the ropes. This should deal the death knell to his hopes. My God, we might actually live to see peace again."

Then he sobered. "But at what a price, as usual. God, how I detest all the killing."

She could only gape at him. She had said it was only men who romanticized war, and had wondered how men like Adam and Filipe would settle down to civilian life afterward. It had never occurred to her that because he was able to adapt himself to the demands of war, that he might still hate its effects, even as she did.

She said unsteadily, unwillingly, "Poor George Austerby—"

His mouth tightened. "I know. I saw Suttler. How bad is he?"

"I think he will—live. But—"

"I know," he said again, quickly. "Don't think of it. Try to forget all the other horrors you have seen as well today. It's the only thing you can do and stay sane."

"Oh, God, yes," she said, momentarily haunted again by the touch of the nightmare. "When I thought you were dead—"

"Don't!" he said again, and his arms tightened almost to pain around her. "Whatever comes, from now on we will face it together. But I really do believe we will be home soon. And in the meantime, we have *this* to cling to." And he set about quite deliberately to prove to her once again that he was very much alive.